THE ONE WHO GOT AWAY

THE ONE WHO GOT AWAY

EROTIC ROMANCE FOR WOMEN

EDITED BY
KRISTINA WRIGHT

CLEIS
PRESS

Published in the United States by Cleis Press, an imprint of Start Midnight, LLC, 101 Hudson Street, 37th Floor, Suite 3705, Jersey City, NJ 07302.

Printed in the United States.
Cover design: Scott Idleman/Blink
Cover photograph: iStockphoto
Text design: Frank Wiedemann
First Edition.
10 9 8 7 6 5 4 3 2 1

Trade paper ISBN: 978-1-62778-177-0

E-book ISBN: 978-1-62778-177-0

Contents

INTRODUCTION: ALWAYS ON MY MIND

We all have...that One, the one who got away. The one we fell for or simply were attracted to, but we never got our heart's desire. That One, but not necessarily *the* One, at least not the first time around. That One who slips into our fantasies late at night when we're feeling melancholy or nostalgic. Maybe we took a chance once upon a time and it simply didn't work out. Maybe we never took the chance...and we wish we had. We all have the name of the one who got away tattooed on our heart, always with us, never forgotten. And sometimes, we get a second chance with that One.

There is something hopelessly romantic about the idea of connecting with a long-lost love. Note I said *idea*. In truth, reconnecting with someone from our past can be...awkward, at best. Of course, it does sometimes work out. I know of two couples who, under very different circumstances, reconnected long after their first meeting and rekindled their passion for each other. In the first case, the couple had dated off and on for years, never quite being on the same page until their paths diverged for a decade and then crossed again. Now they're happily married and raising two children together. In the other case, the two people involved were always attracted to each other but were so very different they both knew they'd never be compatible. Years later, throwing caution to the wind, they took a chance and discovered it was their differences that made them work as a couple. The lesson here is that time has a way of working magic on our lives and our hearts and what might have once seemed foolhardy or even impossible can suddenly turn on a dime at some point in the future.

And so, dear reader, I present you with this luscious collection of second chance stories, about couples who have known each other, and sometimes loved each other, only to be separated by choice or fate. And in every case, something has brought them back together, either deliberately or by happenstance. More than any other anthology I've edited, this one is filled with longing—and hope. Here in these pages, you will find lovers discovering that the heart wants what it wants and is often willing to wait however long it takes to be fulfilled. So much longing, it will make your heart ache, but it isn't unrequited and it doesn't go unfulfilled.

Happy reading, and may the memories of your one who got away be fond. Who knows what the future holds...right?

Kristina Wright
Chesapeake, VA

HOMECOMING

Alex Tobin

Feels strange to be back in Orange County. Like returning to the scene of a crime. I don't remember everything I did when I was here, but it was sex and drugs and punk rock, a laundry list of unpunished misdemeanors and—I'm sure—a felony or two. Still, it's been over a decade. Statutes expire and memories fade.

I sit up, turning to look through the front seats. A SoCal dusk greets me, framed through the windshield, wisps of cloud-like scars on a canvas of purple and orange. I feel dirty and sticky, the beginnings of a headache tapping a heartbeat rhythm through my skull. Back, hip and knee resume their grumbling, a low murmur of constant complaint at my poor posture, at days spent sleeping in my car. The dashboard clock says it's a little after eight. Almost showtime.

It's not quite summer in Anaheim, but in a city where summer's never very far away, that isn't saying much. The sun's out of sight, but the heat of the day still radiates from every surface. I can feel it coming off my car, from the asphalt beneath my feet. I could use a shower, but the best I can hope for is a whore's bath in the restroom of the bar. The Duchess, it's called. I'd say it's seen better days, but I think this is about as good as it ever got for this place. We played here, of course, more than once, on a tiny stage in a tiny room downstairs. I have a vivid memory of opening my eyes between songs and seeing a congregation of expectant faces looking up at me, red with exertion, glistening with sweat, ready for my anger to explode out into that space, to wash over them on a wave of distortion, slam them into one another, into the walls.

Walking in is like going back in time. The bartender's an old punk like me, shirtsleeves rolled up to his biceps, tattoos all the way down to his knuckles.

"I'm Bill Anthony," I tell him.

"Good to meet you, man. Get you a drink?"

"Bourbon. Neat. Beer back."

"Any particular beer?"

"Whatever's cheapest."

"On the house for performers."

"Humor me," I say.

"You're the boss." Then, as he pours, "Gonna be a turnout tonight, I think."

"Yeah?"

"Most of what we get in here is jazz and blues. Good stuff, but the same every night, you know? Soon as we put you on the schedule, people started asking. They remember you."

"Triumphant return of the hometown boy," I say, taking a sip of the bourbon.

"Where you been?"

I down the rest in a couple of quick swallows, drain the beer in turn. "Around," I say.

I never went far, in truth. Just needed to get out of town. The scene got old and then it got dangerous. The vibe changed.

We were all drinking too much. I felt like I was leaving my soul onstage most nights, shouting myself hoarse to be heard over the music, watching the pits get ever more violent. In August of that year, oh-two or oh-three, a kid got his face destroyed at one of our shows, a shattered nose and a broken orbital bone, blood everywhere. The camaraderie that used to be there—the silent code that said you weren't there to hurt anybody else, that if somebody fell you helped them up—was gone, an early casualty of the new suburban angst, of hockey shirts and back-to-front baseball caps and waved middle fingers.

Then Sonny died.

I didn't even know him that well. Lucky Dragon 3 was Jake and me. It was our band. Drummers came and went. Sonny was the fifth and last. He joined the band the same summer that kid got fucked up in the pit, played maybe twenty shows, then got drunk and totaled his car out on the 5 one night, just lost control and drove off the road. Jake called me in the early hours of the morning to give me the news, and we ended it right then and there. He asked me if I wanted to stop and I said yes. We haven't talked since.

I went north. Grabbed some shit from my apartment and took the 101 up the coast. I thought about Canada but never got farther than Seattle, where I bummed around until the money ran out then worked a succession of McJobs, saved up enough money to buy a guitar, and started thinking about the music I'd grown up on, the LA, Orange County, and Bay Area bands of the Eighties and Nineties. I reworked my favorite songs, slowed them down and bluesed them up a little, played some open mics, got some gigs, then started adding in my own material. After a year or so, I didn't have to do the shitty jobs anymore. I slept in my car sometimes, sure, but a choice between eight hours spent sleeping in a beat-up Camaro and eight hours spent pretending to give a shit for minimum wage was no choice at all.

After three drinks and a quick trip to the bathroom to freshen up, people are starting to show up for the gig, and I catch a few glances as I carry my equipment through the bar, a few nudges and "look over there"s. This amount of booze is normally just right for a confidence buzz, but I feel uncomfortably warm and a little nauseous. Only a few of them have made their way downstairs, but I can feel their eyes on me as I set up. It isn't much, just a couple of amps, a microphone, and a stool, but it helps me get focused, takes my mind off the sound of people pulling up chairs, talking amongst themselves.

"All right," I say into the mic, settling myself on the stool. "Not much point sound checking in here. If the levels are off, just yell. My name's Bill Anthony. A long time ago, I had a band called Lucky Dragon 3..." A couple of whoops make me smile despite myself. Nobody's recognized the name since I've been playing alone. "Now it's just me. Same songs, but I got old and stiff and kinda sore, and these days I prefer to do them like this."

I play some Black Flag and TSOL, a couple of my own, then Bad Religion and the Vandals. They're into it, singing along when they know the words, listening politely when they don't, applauding enthusiastically between songs and calling out requests. I usually do Social Distortion's "Story of My Life" at or near the end, but the kid who asks for it is so desperately sincere about hearing it that I go early.

That's when she walks in.

I don't stop playing or fuck up any chords, but I do forget the words to the second verse for long enough that I have to start singing the first again, which isn't the smoothest thing to do when you're playing acoustic and the song's a narrative, but for a few moments, the only word in my head is her name.

She's older, of course, different hair and different clothes and a different way of carrying herself, but I know her face as soon as I see it, and when she makes eye contact and offers me a hesitant smile, I know she came here for me.

Sadie. I don't remember what city we were in, but we were playing an all-ages venue with no bar, supporting some hardcore straight-edge kids who were about as fun as a brick to the face. When we finished our set, we immediately headed out to the parking lot and our van, where we'd left a stockpile of alcohol. As the front man, I usually got more attention than the others, and I was held up chatting to a gang of sweat-soaked teens who wanted to tell me how much they'd enjoyed the show as if I hadn't had the perfect vantage point from which to watch them throwing themselves around with joyful abandon. By the time I got outside, there was already a gathering around the open back doors of the van, where I could see Jake and Connor, our drummer at the time, holding court.

I usually liked these little postmortems, the drinking and the talking and the girls, but it was our third gig in three days, my stage-high was wearing off and I found I wanted nothing more than to get something to eat and then lie down somewhere comfortable, quiet and dark.

"You guys killed it."

I turned my head and there she was, five-feet-nothing of contradictions, this little porcelain doll of a girl, all pale and fragile and absurdly pretty, skin still shiny with sweat, jeans marked with dirt from the dance floor, ill-fitting T-shirt so stretched from being grabbed and pulled in the pit that it hung off one shoulder like a dress.

"Thanks," I said. "You didn't stay for the rest? I hear the headliners have good things to say about orange juice and broccoli."

She smiled and I was done for, all plans for the evening traded in for whatever this girl was doing.

"You don't like them?"

"Their music's okay," I said. "I just don't really...connect with their message. My edge is quite curved."

"So how come you're not drinking with your boys?"

"Tired. Not in the mood for it. Really want a doughnut."

"You sure are punk compared to those straight-edge guys. There's a Krispy Kreme up the street. It might still be open."

"Lead the way, mysterious savior."

"Sadie," she said.

"I'm Billy."

We turned away from the van, heading across the parking lot to the street. I felt better already, feeling the breeze on my face and drying my clothes, sneaking glances at Sadie as we walked.

"Are you here by yourself?" I asked her.

"I came with friends, but they were just hanging out. I don't go to shows to sit and chat, you know?"

"You look like you'd get absolutely killed in a mosh pit."

"I hold my own. It's kind of an advantage. Imagine being the guy that knocked a skinny little girl like me on her ass. It doesn't happen much."

"Never thought about it like that. I'm not in pits that often."

"No," she said, and looked at me with a frankness that made my insides do a lazy backflip. Her eyes were a washed-out blue that was almost gray. "You inspire them, though."

"I scream at people," I said.

"I work at Starbucks."

"Touché."

"Your Krispy Kreme, sir," she said, as we rounded the corner.

"Sadie, I think I love you. I'm buying."

We were just in time. There was nobody else in the store, and the kid behind the counter was clearly annoyed at his closing ritual being interrupted. Disgustingly smitten by the idea of a doughnut filled with custard and dipped in chocolate, I ordered four to go, and we went outside and sat on a low wall in the parking lot, where Sadie looked dubiously into the bag I handed her and then started laughing as I tore into my first doughnut.

"Jesus Christ," she said.

"This is amazing," I said, through a mouthful of doughy sweetness. "This is the greatest thing that's ever happened to me."

"All my preconceptions of what it is to be in a punk band, shattered."

"Try one. These are punk. They're a 'fuck you' to diabetes."

She laughed again, reaching into the bag to pull out a doughnut, holding it between her fingers like it was toxic as she took a tiny bite, eyeing me all the while.

"All right," she said, "it's pretty good. You have custard and chocolate all over your face, dude."

"And that little fucker didn't give us any napkins." I wiped the mess from around my mouth as best I could with my fingers, then sucked them clean.

"Here." Sadie reached over and wiped a bit I'd missed, raised her eyebrows at me, then slipped her own finger briefly into her mouth.

"Can I ask you something?" I felt like my skin was tingling where she'd touched me.

"Sure."

"Do you go to a lot of shows?"

"You mean am I a groupie?" She took a bite out of her doughnut, watching my obvious discomfort as she chewed. "No. I go to a lot of shows, but I get my kicks in the pit, not blowing the bass player. Do you fuck a lot of groupies?"

"I'm not gonna say I never have, but Jake's the reigning champ there." I smiled at her look. "We've got really different stage personas. Some girls like his stoic, relentless rhythm section thing, some like my energy and anger."

"Passion. Not too many people are attracted to anger."

"Not too many people are attracted to guys who talk about how passionate they are, either."

"Touché."

"I guess it kind of extends to who we are when we're not performing. Jake can sleep with three or four different girls in a week and not give it a second thought. I'm always overthinking motives or worrying that they're going to get attached to me or I'm going to get attached to them." I take a bite out of my second doughnut. "Jake says I put women on a pedestal."

"Do you?"

"Maybe. A little. Sometimes."

"I'm not really into the stoic, relentless type." She tossed what was left of her doughnut back into the bag. "And these are too much. Do I have any on my face?"

"Just a little bit."

"Seriously?" She swiped a hand across her mouth. "Still there?"

I nodded, throwing the remnants of my own doughnut into the bag.

"And the little fucker closed the store so I can't go and look in the mirror."

"Here," I said. I leaned in and kissed her lightly, briefly on the side of the mouth. "I think I got it."

"Are you sure?" Her voice was low, her eyes holding mine.

I shook my head and kissed her again, open-mouthed this time. She responded immediately, and I heard the paper bag fall to the ground as she wrapped her arms around my neck, her tongue dancing around mine. I could smell the show on her, the sweat and cigarettes. Beneath that, a cleaner, more intimate scent, soap or shampoo. I put my arms around her waist, slid my hands up under her T-shirt, feeling the warm, smooth skin of her back. She sighed against my lips, let her head fall back a little. I kissed her jaw and the side of her face, her neck and then that exposed shoulder.

"Making out in the Krispy Kreme parking lot," she murmured.

"Does it fit your preconceptions of a guy from a punk band?"

"It's pretty grimy."

"You like that?"

She snorted laughter. "Grimy or that?"

The latter was my hand finding one of her small breasts, bare beneath her T-shirt.

"Whichever," I said, and kissed her again.

"Fuck…" She pushed me away. "Billy, I can't do this. I mean, I can, but I don't want to get you all worked up."

"You're doing pretty badly. What's wrong?"

"I'm on my period."

I exhaled and smiled at her. "I thought you were going to say you had a boyfriend."

"No boyfriend." She brushed my lips with hers. "But you can't fuck me."

"I wasn't going to try and fuck you."

"Why not?" She was grinning, playful.

"Where? Over behind the Dumpsters? The romance."

"Are you pedestaling me?"

"I…no."

"I think you are." She started unbuckling my belt.

"Sadie…"

"Billy."

"You don't have to…"

"Shut up, Billy."

The store was closed and in darkness. We could be seen from the street, but Orange County isn't known for its pedestrian traffic at the best of times, never mind at close to midnight in a dubious part of town, and I doubt anybody in a car would have seen much.

"Sadie…" I said again, this time because she'd undone my pants and pulled down the front of my underwear, her hand warm around my cock as she took me into her mouth.

It didn't take too long. I was already so worked up, reeling from her kisses, her scent, the feel of her breast beneath my hand, that I couldn't have held back if I'd wanted to.

"I'm gonna come," I muttered, in a low, breathless voice.

Sadie went harder, faster, stroking me as her lips moved and her tongue teased. I groaned as I reached my orgasm, my cock twitching and pulsing in her mouth, sweet relief running through my body so that I wanted to slump back on the wall and just close my eyes.

She pushed up off her knees and straddled me, put her arms around me and let her head fall on my shoulder.

"Not to pedestal you," I said, when I'd caught my breath, "but that doughnut is now the second greatest thing that's ever happened to me."

"You're a dork."

"And you're amazing."

She sat back a little, on my thighs, and stared at me for long enough that I started to feel uncomfortable.

"Your guys won't leave without you, will they?" she asked.

"What time is it?"

"After twelve, I bet."

"I probably should get back. The show was over a while ago."

We walked back to the street in a silence that was suddenly awkward. I wasn't sure if I'd said the wrong thing or if she was regretting what had happened. My knuckles brushed hers, and I found myself wanting to grab her hand, to say something.

"Sadie!"

We both looked up. They were waving to her from a car on the other side of the street.

She grinned and waved back. "Hey!"

"Where the fuck have you been?" asked a guy hanging out the passenger side window. "We've been looking everywhere."

She turned back to me. "That's my ride."

"Yeah, okay. Will I see you again?"

She threw herself at me, almost knocking me off-balance, and pressed her mouth to mine in a brief but fervent kiss. "I'll come to a show," she said.

"You'd better."

And she was gone, running across the street to her friends, waving to me from the car as it pulled away, leaving me alone on the sidewalk, feeling like I'd just been punched in the gut.

I get through "Story of My Life," extra verse and all, and I get through the rest of my set without casting too many glances Sadie's way. There are no chairs left, so she leans against the wall at the bottom of the stairs, sipping her drink, watching, listening. At the end of the last song, I look up to find her smiling at me. She mouths two words at me and then disappears up the stairs.

Parking lot.

You can't just ghost out of the room when you're the only act in such an intimate setting. People want to tell you it was a great show, talk about the bands, talk about the scene, ask where you've been and what you've been doing. I keep the conversations as brief as I can, but by the time I get upstairs and out to the parking lot, it's been twenty minutes or more and my stomach's in knots. She's there, though, standing side-on to me, watching the people in the street.

"You know, when you said you'd come to a show..."

She turns. "I'm not the one who left town."

I hold out my arms and she steps into my embrace, presses her face into my chest.

"I'd sort of given up on you by then. That was, what, a year later?"

"Eight months." She looks up at me. Those eyes. "When was the last time you showered, Billy?"

"I mostly go by Bill now."

She wrinkles her nose. "It sounds old. When was the last time you had a good night's sleep, Billy?"

"Shower was a couple of days ago. Sleep, I don't know. I don't always have the money for a motel room. Besides, I thought you liked grimy."

She steps back. "Do you need a place to stay?"

"Need? No." I point at my car.

"Wow," she says, looking back over her shoulder. "That is a punk rock car. Did you have it the last time we met?"

"I did."

"Would you like a place to stay? I have a spare bed and a really nice shower."

"Is there a Mr. Sadie?"

"No. No husbands, boyfriends, roommates or cats. Just me."

"Okay. I've got to pack up my stuff and get my money first. Can you wait a few minutes?"

"I've waited eleven years."

I open my mouth and close it again. "You make this sound really intense when you say that."

"It's not intense?"

"This is where I say the wrong thing and then you get into a random car and drive out of my life."

"Is that what you...?" She laughs a little. "Get your stuff. I'll wait."

It's a couple of trips to grab my equipment and collect a surprisingly thick pile of bills from the bartender. When I'm ready, Sadie hands me a piece of paper with an address scribbled on it.

"Follow me. If you get lost or that car spontaneously crumbles into rust, that's where we're going. Let's not take any chances."

It isn't far, just a couple of exits north. She lives in a gated community, in a townhouse with a beautifully trimmed lawn. When I kill the engine, I'm greeted with the chitter of sprinklers.

"I guess you don't work at Starbucks anymore," I say, climbing out of my car.

"I work for an insurance company," she says. "Executive assistant."

"I feel so fucking grimy right now."

She laughs. "You ain't seen nothing yet."

Her place is three levels, hardwood floors and a stark black and white color scheme. Everything looks new, and—if not expensive—not exactly cheap.

"This is not how I imagined you living."

She falls onto the couch. "You're not the only one. I moved in here a couple of months ago. It feels like a show home or something. I have no idea what I'm doing."

"Well, you're not sleeping in your car."

"There's that. Billy, you look exhausted. Why don't you go take that shower? The bathroom's upstairs."

"I really appreciate this, Sadie."

"I really appreciated hearing you play tonight. Brought back a lot of memories." The way she looks at me reminds me of when she told me I inspired mosh pits.

"I'm glad I came back. And I'm glad you showed up."

I head upstairs to the bathroom, where I undress and look at myself in the mirror, trying to reconcile how I look now with how I looked the night we met. I'm a little leaner than I was then, and I keep my hair a little shorter. There's a severity about my features that never used to be there, a product of my mostly ascetic way of living. I don't look like I just got hit in the face with a decade, though, just tired, worn down.

Sadie's shower is hard to the point of being abrasive. It's wonderful. I turn the heat up as far as I can stand it and let the spray pound my face and my shoulders until I can't take it anymore, then I wash myself, wondering if she still uses the same brand of soap I smelled on her the first time we kissed, a thought that leads very naturally to considering the idea of her in this very shower, naked and glistening, the spray reddening her skin.

"Billy?"

I didn't lock the bathroom door. Didn't even close it. She's standing right outside.

"Yeah?"

"Just making sure you didn't drown in there. It's been a while."

"Sorry. I got a little caught up in how amazingly brutal your shower is. It's like a massage. Can you pass me a towel?"

She steps into the bathroom as I step out the shower, takes the towel off the rail but makes no immediate move to hand it to me.

"And you were so shy the last time," she says.

"Technically, there wasn't a last time."

She looks down at my cock, still semierect from my impure shower thoughts. "Is that for me?"

"Inspired by you."

We start laughing at the same time, and she comes into my arms again, tossing the towel aside as she kisses me, grabbing my cock.

"You're so..." She breathes laughter, warm against my face.

"So what?"

"I don't know, but I want you to take me in the bedroom and do things to me."

I lift her easily off the ground and she wraps her legs around my waist and her arms around my neck, kissing my ear and my neck as I carry her out of the bathroom.

"Second door on the right," she says.

I nudge it open with my foot, carry her in and lay her down on the bed. She watches me as I undo her jeans and pull them down, taking her panties with them. In the light from the hallway, her eyes are half-lidded, her lips wet, slightly parted. I lie down on the bed beside her. This time I kiss her slowly, thoroughly, holding the side of her face, stroking her jawline with my knuckles, then letting my hand stray lower, up underneath her shirt, smoothing the soft skin of her belly. I kiss her neck, sucking lightly, pulling my lips to her skin, grazing her a little with my teeth.

She sighs. "Billy…"

"Mmm?"

"You scared me. You didn't do anything wrong."

"What do you mean?"

"I was scared of how attracted I was to you. We'd known each other less than an hour."

"You don't have to explain."

"I want to."

"You don't have to explain right now."

I cover her mouth with mine, slide my hand down between her thighs, finding her wet. She moans and bites my lip, hips moving as I caress her, hand on the back of my head, grabbing my hair. Her desire, her *lust*, is driving me crazy. I pull away from her hungry mouth, smiling at her as I slide down her body, my hair, still wet from the shower, dripping on her skin, making her laugh as I press my lips to her belly, out to her hip bone and down to her thigh.

"Oh, god…please…" she says, in this desperate whisper that about kills me.

Still, I tease her. I trail kisses up the inside of her thigh, inhale her scent, breathe on her, just brush her with my lips so that she twitches and then half laughs, half sighs as I lick and kiss her other thigh, pull away and then finally press my open mouth to her, exploring with my tongue, finding that hard little bud at the junction of her labia, teasing and playing until she lifts her hips off the bed and grabs my hair again, this time with both hands, urging more.

I listen to her moans, feel the way she reacts, adjusting to chase her pleasure, wanting so badly to get her off. She's tensing and relaxing, writhing on the bed, quieter than she was, her moans strained, like she's struggling. I can feel her getting closer, and I try not to get carried away, try to focus on her.

Finally, she's moving around so much that she's getting away from me. I grab her hands and pin them to the bed at her sides, hold her in place so she can't get away, and that's when she comes, when she stops breathing altogether, her head back and her body rigid, the room silent for a few seconds until the air rushes out of her in a long, low moan and she falls back.

I lie beside her and she smiles at me, breathing deeply, hair damp with sweat.

"I love what you do," she says, a few minutes later. "The romance of it. I love the way you don't give a fuck. The first time I saw you onstage, you blew me away. When I came up to you outside, it was just to say that I thought you were awesome, that the show was great, but I just felt so fucking drawn to you. I mean, lust, yeah, but you have something about you, like you know something the rest of us don't. It scared the shit out of me. I worked so hard and made so many sacrifices going to college and working that stupid fucking job to make ends meet, and sitting on your lap in the parking lot of fucking Krispy Kreme, I felt like I could just get in that van with you and never miss any of it."

"I'd have let you."

"I know. The way you looked at me made it real, like we were about to do something crazy. I had to talk myself down, let that rational voice that knows how much guys love blow jobs take over." She pulls closer to me, puts her head on my chest. "I thought about it a lot, but by the time I plucked up the courage to come and see you again, the band had broken up. You were gone."

"I'm here now," I say, "and it's a hell of a lot better than sleeping in my car. This is the first time in a long time I haven't been in any pain."

"Maybe you should stay awhile," she says, sitting up, crossing her arms over her chest and taking off her shirt. "See how the other half lives."

I smile, thinking of a song I might play, a song I might write. "Maybe I will."

AGAIN

Renee Luke

*J*ones, Mace

Drawing in a deep breath, Cyrena Howell tenderly traced the name on her manila file with her fingertip. How many Mace Joneses could there be, and how many would actually be on base near the tiny Southern California town where they both grew up? It had to be *him*. She closed her eyes against the sudden burn of moisture, but that didn't stall the barrage of memories. A lump tightened her throat.

Shaking her head, she opened her eyes and willed away the threat of tears. She didn't have time for memories of a dozen years ago, of young love and unkept promises of forever. Swallowing down the lump, she pulled her shoulders back and tore her gaze away from his name. She'd become accustomed to and accomplished at suppressing the yearning for shoulda, woulda, couldas. She'd spent years mastering the technique of giving up what she wanted to do for all the things that needed doing.

Right now, she needed to do her damn job, not stare at her

patient's name like a crushing teenager. Trembling hands be damned, she twisted the handle and silently stepped into the exam room where he was waiting.

He was sitting on the treatment table, his head bent down as he scrolled through pages on his cell phone. He hadn't noticed her. Except for the width of his shoulders and breadth of his chest, he was just as she had seen him last. He wore his green cammies and jungle boots, his hair cleanly shaven into a tight fade, his skin the same tempting milk chocolate.

Her heart thumped hard in her chest, her lungs burning as she held her breath. He might look like the boy who'd left her over a decade ago, but he wasn't.

He'd come home a man.

Her body responded like a woman. A woman who'd known the tenderness of his touch, the gentleness of his kisses, and had set an unattainable standard for every other lover since. Her nipples puckered. Every cell warmed in memory.

His arms were thick, heavily corded with a shadow of a tattoo teasing the edge of his sleeve. And scars? She narrowed her eyes and squinted at his arm. If only she hadn't been distracted by his name and had taken a moment to read over his file before entering, so she'd be aware of the extent of his injuries. She tightened her hand around her folder to keep from reaching for him, her fingers itching to trace the scars. To erase them.

To fix him.

"Mace," she said. She hadn't meant it to sound so hushed, like a bedroom whisper.

His gaze lifted to hers, recognition instant. A moment—just a fleeting moment—passed, but it stretched between them, the silence full of words needing to be said, but unspoken. His dark eyes seemed to melt and return to solid in the span of a heart-beat.

"Cyrena."

She saw his throat work as if saying her name had been diffi-cult.

Saying her name seemed to jar him and he jumped to his feet to stand by the exam table. But the movement cost him. Cyrena didn't miss the slight wince or the look of pain that marred his brow, even as he stood steadily. She was always telling her patients that they were injured and didn't need to get up when she came in, but it seemed they always did regardless of her reminders.

Mace was clearly here because he was injured. He didn't need to stand for her, but he was a Marine and standing when a woman entered seemed to go hand in hand with wearing the uniform. Her gaze traveled down his body. He wore that uniform well.

"What are you doing—" they both began at once.

He smiled. *Oh damn*, the same lopsided grin on those same lickable lips that had seduced her out of her virginity. Cyrena wanted to turn around and run. No, she wanted to strip off her scrubs and fuck away the years on the exam table. Her pussy was damp. Her inner thighs ached.

He lifted his left arm toward her. "You first."

She shook her head and cleared her throat. "Was a stupid question. You were injured and are here for therapy." She opened the file and glanced down. He'd taken some shrapnel to his right shoulder and upper arm and had had several surgeries trying to repair the damage.

She glanced back at him, looking all delicious and sexy in his fatigues. Her assistant was supposed to have asked him to remove his shirt and put on an exam gown, but Mace was still fully clothed. She skimmed down his chart. "Two weeks post-surgery." She glanced at him and warmth spread across her cheeks. "Are you able to remove your shirt?"

He chuckled. "You haven't seen me in years and you want

me naked just like that? Whatever you say, doctor." With his left hand, he reached back and shrugged out of his shirt, tossing it to the chair in the corner.

"I don't. I mean, I'm not. Um, I mean, I don't." Her cheeks burned as she stumbled over her words. If he hadn't been grinning at her with a smirk gleaming in his eyes, she'd have put the manila folder to use and fanned her face. Taking a breath, she pretended like that hadn't happened and approached him.

She put the file on the table. Glancing up at him, she said, "Please sit down." When he complied, she touched his shoulder around the area where the skin was red and puckered from the recent removal of stitches. He flinched and she could tell he was holding his breath.

"I'm not a doctor," she finally said. Her words were soft as she continued to examine the two different surgery sites and a dozen other smaller scars where the skin was still healing. "I'm a physical therapist. I can't fix your arm, but I can help you make it usable again."

Cyrena tried to think of him as any other patient. Tried to treat him like any other. But he wasn't. Mace Jones was the only man she'd ever loved. She didn't want to do exercises and ice, electrical muscle stimulation and heating pads. She wanted to kiss the marred skin and run her fingers over every inch of his warm body. She wanted to show him she had loved him all these years. That she loved him still.

She cleared her throat, but the tight, dry feeling persisted. "Lift your arm to the side until you feel pain." Emotion welled in her eyes, but she chastised the tears away.

He lifted his arm to about a forty-five degree angle before his muscles tightened, his body reacting to the pain. "You went away to school?"

It was a pointed question and she knew what he was really asking. *You went away for school, but you couldn't go away for me?* She shook her head. "Not at first. Not until"—her voice cracked—"not until the girls graduated high school and Grandpa died."

"I'm sorry," he said.

Cyrena could hear the emotion in his tone, the sincerity. Averting her face, she continued her exam, ignoring the two silent tears as they slid hot down her cheeks. Her chest burned. Her nostrils and eyes burned with the pain of holding back the long overdue sobs. She spoke despite the rasp of sorrow. "Squeeze this ball," she said, and handed him a small red ball. "It may not seem like it's doing much, but you're wounded so we've got to take this slow."

He accepted the ball with his right hand and began to squeeze. "You're wounded, too."

The depth of tenderness in his voice nearly broke the shred of control damming the flow of tears. "I'm not." *A lie,* her heart screamed.

"You are," he whispered, grabbing her arm with his left hand. He gave a little tug, but it didn't take much force to have her step in his direction. He pulled her closer, between the *V* of his legs. "You are, baby, or you wouldn't be crying."

"I'm not." She forced the words past the lump in her throat. Inhaling was a mistake. It carried the scent of him, of sunshine and ocean, of Ivory soap and wind, of masculinity and strength. She ached for his strength. Yearned for it.

"Nah?" His hand left her arm and he touched her cheek with his thumb. "Then what's this?" he asked, holding the captured tear between them.

A sob broke, but Cyrena tucked her bottom lip into her mouth and refused another its freedom. She could feel the small exercise ball press to the back of her leg as he used his wounded arm to urge her forward.

"Come here." He put his left hand to her cheek, then spread

his strong fingers into curls she'd had a hard time securing into a hair band that morning. He pulled her closer. For a moment she thought he was going to kiss her, but he didn't. He rested his forehead against hers. And closed his eyes.

He held her there, their bodies inches apart, his injured hand keeping her from stepping away, his other hand tangled in her hair. She could feel his breaths on her cheeks and could smell the saltiness of tears causing her to wonder if they were her own. Or his.

His voice was low and raw when he finally spoke. "I shouldn't have left you."

Even with all his strength and power, she didn't miss the pain in his tone. It was so easily recognizable because it was as poignantly deep as her own. "You had to go." She reached up and touched his face. He didn't open his eyes, but turned his head and pressed a tender kiss to her palm. "You had to," she whispered.

She gulped. Mace had been in foster care most of his life and had aged out of the system two weeks before graduation. He had no one but her and nowhere to go. The military had been his best and, he'd said, his only option. He had enlisted on his eighteenth birthday and left for boot camp three weeks later. That was the last time she'd seen him. Twelve years ago.

"You should've come with me." He spoke against her hand, but she felt the vibration of his words pulse through her body.

Swallowing down the pain, she replied, "I couldn't. You know I couldn't leave when the girls still had two years of high school. All their friends were here. And I couldn't leave after Grandpa got diagnosed with lung cancer. He took care of us when Mama bailed. I had to take care of him."

Her mama bailing had been how she'd first met Mace. He'd been at the same short-term foster care when on her thirteenth birthday her mama decided she didn't want to raise children anymore, especially not teens. Mace had been there waiting for another long-term placement. She and her younger sisters had only been there over the weekend until Grandpa could claim them legally.

He'd taken over being the parent from then on. And she'd taken on being the caretaker right before she got out of high school. She'd planned on leaving with Mace when he'd enlisted. A cancer diagnosis had changed everything.

"Cyrena, I enlisted to take care of you. To take care of us."

A tremor slid down her back. He'd had big dreams and made bigger promises as a teen. Her lids drifted closed, the memories almost too painful to bear, because despite his promised dreams, reality had held her underwater until she nearly drowned. She had thrown herself into mothering her younger sisters and nursing her ailing grandfather. She'd put every bit of herself into them so she wouldn't have to think of Mace. That he was gone and might never come back. At least not alive. That without him she'd never again be whole.

But now he was here. He was here, again. She took a breath. "I couldn't go with you, Mace. I had to take care of my family. The girls deserved to graduate high school with their friends. Like we did. Grandpa needed me. His last days weren't easy and..." Her voice trailed off. She couldn't say anything else. Another word and she'd be weeping in his lap.

He lifted his head from hers and she nearly tumbled into him, surprised by the absence of his support. "Ah, I'm sorry," she said as she lost her balance and grabbed his shoulders to keep from falling. She could feel him flinch under the contact, but he didn't move away.

Mace was hurting all right, but it didn't have a damn thing to do with his shoulder. Hell no, he'd gotten used to that pain, had figured out how to deal with it. What he hadn't been prepared for was how quickly he'd gone hard, rocked up and aching, seeing Cyrena standing there staring at him, all moist eyed and lush lipped. She was thicker now than he remembered, but shit, she was perfect. She wore scrubs, but the square-shaped clothes didn't do a thing to hide her luscious curves.

She'd been shocked to see him. He knew she would be. He might have stayed away from her for more than a decade, but that didn't mean he'd stayed away. He'd known she was a physical therapist and had even taken leave to stand in the shadows when she graduated college. He had promised her he would take care of her and he was a Marine, a man of his word. She wouldn't go with him and had ended their relationship, saying she couldn't hold him back, but that didn't mean he had forgotten about his promises.

When he'd been injured, so severely he'd wished for death more than once during his slow recovery and return to the States, there was only one thing he feared. That he couldn't keep his word. Couldn't return to Cyrena and make sure she was okay. And when he began to heal, the only thing he could think about was getting better quickly and getting back to her.

He'd planned this. Even pre-surgery, he knew as soon as he could go to therapy, he'd go see her. The time had come. He'd thought he was prepared to see her, and he was. But he hadn't been prepared for his utter, unabated need. And now she was here, in his arms. More than a decade be damned, this was exactly where she was supposed to be.

Mace slid his hand from her glorious curls, smoothing down her arm until her left hand was in his. He didn't look down, just rubbed his thumb across her fingers. He hadn't realized he'd been holding his breath until relief allowed its escape. No ring.

With her hand still in his, he tugged her onto his lap, using her surprise to his advantage.

"Mace!" She wiggled, trying to get up, but he pulled her

forward until she was forced to spread her knees and straddle him on the exam table. He knew the second she felt his hard dick under her ass. She went still, then seemed to melt against his chest. "Mace," this time a mirrored whisper of his own need.

Damn she felt good touching him, all soft and sweet and womanly curves. She smelled of springtime flowers and exotic rain. He dreamt of holding her like this, but it wasn't enough. He needed more. Needed to be skin to skin. Needed to be naked and inside her. Needed to fuck her until her heart was exposed in her cries of pleasure.

Until it was his name she moaned as she melted around him.

"Cyrena, I'm wounded." He pressed his mouth to her neck, to the tender skin below her ear.

"I know." The words were spoken so softly he felt them as much as heard them. She relaxed into him, slanting her head to the side so he could kiss her skin.

He smoothed his mouth along her racing pulse, the echo of his own. She moaned and grasped on to him, one arm around his left shoulder, the other around his waist. She tightened her fist into his T-shirt, holding on.

He moved upward, kissing along the shell of her ear, biting down a little on the fleshy lobe. She whimpered and wiggled against his hard dick. With her legs spread, he could feel the heat of her pussy and he had to fight the urge to turn caveman and shove his hand down her pants to see if she was as wet as he wanted her to be. Needed her to be.

Her ass was soft against him, but she was hurting him. Damn cammies had fit fine before she'd walked in. But now his erection was throbbing against her softness, held in check by scrubs and fatigues. The pain of not being able to claim her rivaled the injuries on his shoulder.

"I'm home now, baby."

Her eyes were closed, long lashes resting against latte cheeks, but she sought his mouth with hers. "I know, and I'll take care of you," she whispered against his lips.

Damn, she tasted like home. Sweet like warm honey, intoxicating like a double shot of Hennessy. And he could taste her silent tears. *Never again. Never, ever again*, he vowed, would she cry anything but happy tears. He deepened the kiss, pressing his tongue into the sultry depth of her mouth, claiming what was his.

What had always been his.

She responded quickly, eagerly touched her tongue to his and he damn near came in his pants. A couple more minutes and he'd have her naked and fucked senseless on the treatment table.

Mace drew from years of training and discipline and reined himself in. He pulled back from the kiss, pressing his mouth to hers a few more times as he eased back. She was breathing heavily, her eyes filled with a yearning so deep he almost felt guilty making her wait. Shit, this might have been the time, but it sure as hell wasn't the place, he realized, glancing around the small glass-walled room, their only privacy the pulled curtain.

"Cyrena, you said we had to take my therapy slow." He kissed her mouth when she nodded. "We can take this as slowly as you want, baby, but I want us."

"Mace."

"I'll date you. Romance you. Fast. Slow. Whatever you need. Just let me see you again."

She was smiling but he didn't miss the way her body trembled in his arms. She nodded and pressed her lips to his as she spoke, "Yes. When?"

The world had shifted. It'd been off kilter, but now it was upright again. Mace grinned as he put down his beer and grabbed his remote control. Things weren't perfect. Not yet. His arm was still fucked up and he never could sleep. Too many nightmares.

Too many ugly dreams of desert sand stinging his eyes, of blaring blasts ringing in his ears, of men in his unit crying out as death claimed them.

Shit, even ten thousand miles away, back home in his small ocean-side town, some things you just didn't get over. Kicking his feet onto the coffee table, he flicked from ESPN to the NFL Network. They were talking about the kickoff of training camps, but the updates were just background noise. A distraction.

Taking a breath, he closed his eyes and leaned back. No, things weren't perfect, but they sure as hell were getting better. He'd spent too many years in the desert. Too many tours overseas at war. More than a decade being a soldier and not nearly enough time just being a man.

Not that he hadn't dated. He had. He'd even been in a couple of short-term relationships, but he'd never been able to really commit to any of the women in his life. Hell no, not when his heart had already been claimed by the first and only woman he had ever loved.

Opening his eyes, he glanced across the room at the metal locker he'd been issued at boot camp. Once it held all his gear, but now it held all of his pre-Marine possessions. As a foster kid, there hadn't been much, just a trash bag of clothes, a couple of varsity football patches, a yearbook and the promises he'd made to his girl so many years ago.

He grinned and closed his eyes again. That locker held his past and all his hopes of a future.

Taking a deep breath, Mace tried to tune in to what was being said about his Chargers, but it was damned hard to focus on football when he'd been half-hard for a couple of weeks straight and the woman responsible for all his discomfort would be over in a few hours.

"Cyrena," he mumbled, tossing the remote aside and grabbing his hard dick. He'd left behind a girl and returned to a woman. She still had the wild sunshine and dusk hair that was more frizz than curls, and liquid amber eyes that held both innocence and too much pain. The same supple lips and smile.

But her body had filled out, her breasts were bigger, her hips wider, her thighs thicker. It'd been a few weeks of yearning and cold showers, a few weeks of both physical therapy and torture. He'd seen her three times a week for therapy. She'd worked out his shoulder and arm; he'd followed directions but could only think of spreading those lush thighs and sinking into her wet pussy. Of working *her* out.

He clenched his jaw, need sharp and raw. Drawing in a breath, he tried to shake his lust. It'd been a few weeks of therapy and dinners, of walks and kisses, of teasing and sleeping alone. He'd had e-fucking-nough.

Cyrena Howell was his and tonight he meant to make her know it.

He suppressed a groan and tried to focus on the TV. He'd chill now, watch some football updates and in an hour he'd get up and set his scene for seduction. The candles, wine and flowers were waiting in the kitchen.

She'd knocked three times already and the only thing Cyrena could hear was the television blaring about football. Her heart thumped hard in her chest. Could something have happened to him? His shoulder was making progress, but maybe there was more wrong than he had told her about.

She tried the door and found it unlocked, so she let herself in. She'd just gotten him back in her life. Her body ached in fear just thinking of losing him again. The bungalow was small, but clean and orderly. The front door opened into the main living room and as soon as she stepped inside she saw Mace sleeping upright on the couch. His right elbow was propped up on a pile of pillows, a beer had shed condensation on the side table, and the remote had been tossed aside.

She noticed everything, but only saw him. He wore black basketball shorts that rode low on his hips, and nothing else. His chocolate skin appeared rich and warm in the shadows of the sunset in the western sky. His body was perfect even with the scars on his shoulder. She stepped closer, wanting to touch him. She clenched her fists, her fingertips tingling to smooth across the Devil Dog tattoo on his shoulder, to trace the silver puckered wounds, to follow the chiseled dips and valleys of his corded muscles. To follow the lines across his pecs, to his abs.

To follow the trail of dark hair that dipped from below his belly button beneath the waistband of his shorts. His left hand clenched the material and she could tell he was holding his dick. And he was hard. She trembled, her nipples pulling tight with desire, moisture dampening her pussy.

She stepped closer. How easy it would be to straddle his waist, pull down his shorts and ride him awake. A throb started in her clit. Her heartbeat pulsed in her ears, need pushing her forward. She stepped closer, biting down on her bottom lip to silence her whimper of need. As if to match her racing pulse, she saw his erection throb beneath the material of his shorts.

Smiling, she glanced up toward his face. His eyes were hooded, but he was awake. Watching her. The cocky lopsided grin that always freed the butterflies in her belly was smeared across his lips.

"Hi," she whispered, the heat on her cheeks spreading, feeling both embarrassed to have been caught gawking at him and turned on by his reaction.

"Hi, yourself."

"I knocked." She glanced in the direction of the door, and then back at him. "I got worried when you didn't answer."

His grin widened. "I'm good."

Her gaze dropped back to his lap. "I can see that."

His hand tightened around his length, his fingers holding the thin material to him. "I was just thinking about you."

Cyrena laughed and took a step forward. "You were sleeping."

He shifted on the couch and one of the pillows under his right elbow tumbled to the floor. "Yeah, well maybe I dozed off for a minute, but I was," he worked his dick in his hand as if the cloth didn't exist, "thinking about you."

She tried to bite back the moan, but it escaped low and needy, and her voice was breathy when she spoke. "You were? About me? What were you thinking?"

He laughed, and held out his hand to her. "Come here, I'll show you."

Taking his hand, she allowed him to draw her closer, tugging her down to him. "Mace," she giggled, spreading her legs and straddling his lap, her knees forced apart over his thighs.

"You feel that?"

He shifted his body, forcing his hard dick up against her. Her sundress floated around her, her legs naked beneath, a thin strap of lace covering her tightly manicured curls.

She shifted her hips, riding up the length of him, wishing he wasn't wearing shorts and that she'd left off her panties. "I feel you," she murmured, silken moisture seeping from her core, her thighs trembling in need.

"That's what you do to me."

She wiggled, rubbing her body against him. Between moans, she whispered, "So Mace," and shifted, putting her hand between them and wrapping her fingers around his rocked-up length, "are you getting rid of these shorts, or are we going to dry fuck like we did when we were teenagers?"

He roared with laughter, the vibration making a hum against her clit. He shifted, his hand reaching for her, strong fingers wrapping around the back of her neck and into her hair. He dragged her forward until her breasts were smashed between them.

His timbre was rough as he said, "We're not teenagers anymore, Cyrena." His right hand moved between them, his fingers sinking between her swollen lips. "And there's no way we can dry fuck when you're already soaking wet."

Cyrena shivered, but Mace didn't wait for a reply. His mouth was on hers, claiming any words that she'd have spoken. His lips were soft but demanding. Demanding but gentle. He angled his head, deepening the kiss, his tongue entering her depths, touching, licking, tasting.

Her eyes drifted closed, her body going liquid under his command. The thick erection pressed against her ass and she needed it inside her. Needed his solid dick pounding into her, releasing everything she'd held back for over a decade. She opened her mouth and kissed him back, meeting his tongue with hers, kissing and nipping and nibbling.

Frantic now, her body was on fire, cold need prickling along her back. She shoved at his basketball shorts, pushing them down, breathing a sigh of relief when his engorged deep-purple head was stripped of clothing. She didn't break the kiss, and accepted his groan into her mouth as she touched her fingertips to his satin flesh.

"I need you, Mace." She kissed the corner of his mouth, moved across his jaw to his ear and whispered, "I've always needed you."

"Dayummm, baby." A low rumbled moan poured from his lips, every muscle in his body coiled beneath his skin. "I'm here." Without warning, he flipped them so she was on her back on the sofa, her sundress billowed around her waist, her legs spread as he settled between them. The rest of the pillows tumbled to the floor.

He held himself up with his left hand as he used his right to shrug the rest of the way out of his shorts, but she didn't miss the tense look on his brow. When his shorts were gone, he reached between them and pushed the thin lace panties to the side, his fingers entering her, stroking out the moisture, his thumb pressing circles against her clit.

And then his plum-shaped head was there instead of his fingers, an inch inside of her, pushing her lips apart to accept him. Still supporting himself with his left arm, he grabbed her thigh over his right and lifted it, spreading her body farther. A rough growl escaped from the back of his throat.

"Mace, don't, you'll hurt yourself."

He chuckled, but the sound was strained. "Baby, I'm gonna hurt if I don't do this." And then he thrust in with no further warning.

Cyrena closed her eyes against the rush of emotion, and relaxed her legs as all those rocked-up inches of his erection thrust into her. Deep, so deep she felt him press against her womb, her heart, her soul. When he was all the way in, she ground her clit into him, shaking as her body stretched around him, as heat poured to her toes, as arousal elongated her nipples.

Gulping for air, she remained still for a moment allowing the connection between them to flow through her. Remained still so the tingle of climax would subside just long enough for her to get fucked right.

"Mace," she cried out, but was silenced as his lips covered hers, her scream captured in his mouth.

He fucked slowly at first, long full strokes that ground into her body, then slow withdrawals and tender returns. Her legs shook, her clit throbbed. She tightened her fist into the back of the couch as he worked his length into her again and again. In and out, the movements filled with tenderness. Tension coiled in her gut, her skin prickling with impending climax.

She arched her back, rising to meet his downward thrusts. And then the movements changed, became frenzied as he drove hard into her, his muscles tightly corded, strained against each movement. She shifted as he thrust in, his dick hitting just the right spot. Her control imploded, every muscle shivering as she climaxed onto his dick. The pleasure of orgasm chased away what lingered of regret.

He released her mouth, his head falling back, his dark eyes hooded. "Baby," he mumbled, his jaw tight, his body tense, "Cyrena, this is right." And he emptied into her, his body shaking violently as he came.

He came hard, filling her with his hot sticky seed and she accepted him, cradled between her legs, their bodies one. He collapsed against her, his face coming to rest against her breasts, his breathing fast and heavy.

After a couple of minutes he released her leg that had been draped over his right elbow. "Doc, I think you may have to ice me," he said with a chuckle.

Cyrena laughed. She couldn't help it. She wanted this. *Him.* Had always wanted it. The last few weeks had simply been a reminder of fate, a fate that brought them together one weekend at a children's receiving home.

"I'll ice you, soldier, but you have to feed me first. I worked all day, and I'm pretty sure you promised me dinner."

"Damn." He laughed as he backed away from her, his dick still half hard as he withdrew. "I had plans for this," he said as he walked naked across the room, his body shimmering with sweat, his dick wet from her climax.

He returned a few minutes later with candles and flowers and chocolates. "I planned on seducing you tonight."

She smiled. "Guess I ruined your plans."

He winked. "Yeah, baby, you did. You'll have to make it up to me."

She pushed her dress down as she sat down and accepted the box of chocolates, nodding as she plopped one into her mouth.

"There's something else." He walked to his metal footlocker and withdrew a small blue velvet box. "I'll be whatever you need me to be, baby, but I'm not going back to active duty. I can be here for you. You want to date, we'll date." He strolled, naked, back to the sofa and went down on one knee before her. "You want a boyfriend, I'll be your boyfriend, but what I want is for you to be my wife." He opened the box and handed it to her.

"Mace." Her hands were trembling as she accepted it from him.

"It's not much, Cyrena. I bought it before I left for boot camp, when I thought you were coming with me. But if you say yes, I'll double the size of that rock. Triple it. Whatever you want."

She swallowed, the lump in her throat making it hard to speak. Her hands shook as she took the ring from the box and put it on her own finger. "The ring is perfect the way it is." The tears were flowing now, the memories of promises holding the right future.

He laughed and twined their fingers. "So you're mine again."

"Always."

POLYGLOT

Skylar Kade

Yes, that's it. That's how she licked me." I moaned and thrust my hips up against Sergio's flexing tongue. I continued narrating. It never failed to get my lover so hot that he would fuck me as soon as I came. "We were in the greenroom of the auditorium after her rehearsal, bra straps slipping off our shoulders before the door could even close behind us."

He slipped two fingers, then three, inside me. I was wet, ready.

Nostalgic, though that was new. Something about the impending ten-year college reunion made all those long-ago memories more poignant. Sharper, cutting against the edges of my current life. Sergio curled his fingers against my G-spot, the hot spot that Ekaterina had introduced me to over and over again in our thousand days together. "Harder, deeper." Ekaterina's fingers had been long and slim, perfect for violin, so perfect she'd left everything in New York right after graduation for the chance to play with the Mariinsky Theater Orchestra in Saint Petersburg.

I looked down my body, noting the stretch marks and softness that hadn't lingered on my frame as a coed. But Sergio, his muscled, tawny shoulders spreading my pale thighs, loved every inch. "You are so beautiful, *amore*," he whispered, like he did every chance he got. Like I was Christmas and birthdays and summer vacation wrapped up, with an extra thirty pounds for good measure.

Despite my initial fears, it never got old to hear. Especially now that we were solid, strong. Those first years had been hell, when *you are so beautiful* was as close to an apology as he ever got.

While his fingers undulated in time with his tongue, Sergio crawled his other hand up my body to lay over my heart. "Mine, my Katie," he uttered, before returning to my pleasure.

"Yours."

When he slowed, I took the unspoken cue and continued the story, not that he hadn't heard some version of it a hundred times in the years since he'd discovered my Sapphic past. "We were stark naked and she had me on the vanity counter, ready and waiting when the door opened"—I gasped as Sergio danced his tongue over a particularly sensitive spot—"and the first chair trombonist stood in the doorway, gaping at us."

I twined my fingers with Sergio's where they lay on my chest. The memory pushed me closer to the edge. "He'd left his sweatshirt in there, swear to god, like it was straight out of *Penthouse*."

He knew this part well by now. "Lucky boy."

The dark pleasure crawled up from the past and I shuddered. "Oh hell, lucky me. Do you have any idea how talented brass players are with their mouths? What four hands can do?"

"Total overload." He thrust three fingers in my pussy, suctioned his mouth on my clit, and drew circles around my anus with his pinky, blowing me past all recollections of other lovers. Shocks exploded from my core out to the top of my head and tips of my fingers and soles of my feet.

He drew out the pleasure, gliding his fingers through the wetness between my legs, before he thrust into me. "If we had a woman here, now," he said, "you'd let her lick your pussy, wouldn't you? Dirty girl."

"Yes," I hissed, writhing against his penetration. Even after all this time, his size still jolted me. So much bigger than the toys Ekaterina and I played with. So hot and alive.

But his filthy words did me in every time. He told me all the ways he'd take me and another woman, never specifically Trina but we both knew who we were picturing. I came again and he followed me, panting and gasping as the phantom third partner faded away.

In the bright morning light, as the minutes counted down before we really—truly this time—had to get ready for work, Sergio pulled me flush against his body. Despite the long hours he worked as a translator for the UN, he'd maintained the fit, athletic body that had originally caught my eye at an unofficial holiday work party. His voice, that syrupy Italian accent, was second.

His passion for life hooked me, though. Pulled me out of the timid shell I had crawled into after graduation. After heartbreak.

"You still love her, don't you?"

I could never lie to him. And what was the point? He understood love wasn't some finite resource. Hell, he'd taught me that. "Of course I do. Just as I'll always love you."

Dashing as ever in his charcoal-gray suit and olive-green tie, Sergio looked every inch the European playboy. One hand tangled with mine as we walked while the other threaded through his hair.

"Don't be nervous. It's just dinner." We passed one of the college's scattered campus buildings, heading for a restaurant-slash-bar-slash-club we used to crash at during late nights studying or, more often, partying. Our alma mater had to rent the place out to hold all the nostalgia that would accompany the gathered alums.

"I never understood class reunions." His shiny dress shoes clipped against the brick sidewalk. If I were any shorter, I'd have to jog to match his pace.

"And your family reunion? You think that was a bundle of laughs, only understanding a fraction of what they were saying?"

He paused and turned me in his arms, then dipped me back in the fading sunlight. "You loved it, *amore*. Two weeks in Italy? All that home-cooked food? And my family adored you." His brow wrinkled, and he swooped in for a kiss. "Especially Dominic. He adored you too much."

I laughed, remembering the teasing flirtation I'd gotten from one of Sergio's cousins. "Well maybe you'll snag a dance with the former Pi Beta Phi president."

Once inside, the voices of all my former classmates echoed off the walls. We signed in with minimal fuss, and headed to the name badge desk.

I froze. There, spotlit under the angry fluorescent lighting, was The Name.

Ekaterina Dobrev.

Like it was the same as the hundred other tags. Like it didn't just wreck my fucking world.

Sergio sensed it. One look at my face, then at my line of vision, and I didn't have to say a word. No, my lover swept an arm around my back, supportive and supporting as my knees wobbled. He nuzzled against my neck. "It's okay *ciccina*. Would you like to leave?"

"I need a drink." His kiss against my temple fortified. "Hopefully the liquor is better than it was in college. I'm about ten years too old for rail vodka."

Three screwdrivers, some close dancing and the throbbing light show let me drift away from the badge. I had even caught up with a dozen former classmates in the packed restaurant, watching Sergio try not to smirk as they all talked a big game about how successful they had become. I did my usual, asking questions and listening as people talked in circles.

Finally, as a lull hit the crowd, Sergio returned with a bottle of water. Good thing, because the room was getting a little blurry around the edges. I gulped down half the bottle before a Nineties throwback came on and Sergio pulled me again to my feet. "One more dance."

There wasn't space for a tango or cha-cha or any of the ballroom dances he'd taught me, but swaying against his lithe, muscled body infused me with all his warmth. His hands stroked up and down my back. I caught sight of the class president dancing with the former Goth queen, and the champion lacrosse player exchanging terse words with his trophy wife. Past and present overlaid until déjà vu hit me like vertigo.

And then, like I had summoned her from memory, Ekaterina stood backlit in the doorway. I knew it in my gut, didn't need to see her face or read her name badge.

Buzzing kicked up in my ears and I clutched Sergio. "She's here." My voice sounded more like our ancient pack-a-day neighbor's than my own. "I...I've got to..."

Though I caught the tail end of Sergio's warning that he would give me a five-minute head start before coming to find me, I didn't reply. We'd done this before, knew the routine. I got some time alone to get my head on straight and figure out whether I needed to rant or breakdown or cuddle or fuck it away, and Sergio didn't have to deal with the crazy headspace I was in. He would show up soon and put the pieces of me back together.

I pushed through the side door off the dance floor that opened into a small walkway at the side of the building. Heat leached off my skin and the faint smell of Saucer Magnolias and cab exhaust gave me something else to focus on.

I had done what I set out to do: make an appearance. Part masochism, part voyeurism...like everyone else who attended their reunions. Watching the past from a safe distance was one thing; letting it sucker punch you, another entirely.

The door behind me slammed open. "Took you long enough. Ready to go?" I turned and swallowed thickly. It wasn't Sergio.

"I thought I saw you leave, *kotonok.*"

I was sucked into the past, kicking and screaming. Ekaterina hadn't aged, aside from elegant laugh lines around her eyes. Same tall, whip-thin frame, white-blonde hair, and eyes so blue they almost burned. Words stuck to the roof of my mouth, part vodka-thick tongue, part shock. How many dirty conversations with Sergio had me reliving this very reunion? Dammit, she even smelled the same. A whiff of Love's Baby Soft reached my nose and I wanted to bury my face against Trina's neck.

"I'm so glad you're here. I..." Ekaterina tugged at a lock of hair, just like she had when cramming for a test in calculus—not her forte. "I'm sorry, Katie. So fucking sorry." She closed the distance and before I could process, Ekaterina had me wrapped in her long, muscled violinist arms, like she'd read my mind.

Tears burned my eyes, but I waited for Ekaterina to finish. I could feel the rest of what my ex wanted to say, like a word caught on the tip of my tongue.

"Leaving you was a mistake."

And my world crumbled, unraveled back to that moment of divergence. *Nothing is more important than my career, not even you.* The words hurt as much now as they did when Ekaterina had hurled them during our last big fight. "Don't say that." I hissed the words out and my breath raised more of Ekaterina's scent, potent as airborne fentanyl.

I saw hair prickle up on Ekaterina's neck and braced myself. In an instant, I was back against the brick wall with Trina looming over me. Our hands were twined and locked above my head against the side of the building. "Not married?"

I shook my head, unable to explain that what I had with Sergio didn't need the blessing of church or government.

Ekaterina's little sigh-growl vibrated through my body, then her lips covered mine.

Bliss. Softer than Sergio's, Trina's kiss was like sinking into a familiar mattress. Comforting, like home. Then her tongue darted out and the familiar taste of orange Tic Tacs invaded. I needed her more than my next breath, like I'd spent the past ten years doing nothing but waiting for her to return.

But I hadn't. I was turned on and so furious that she'd waltz back in and pick up like she hadn't eviscerated me. I'd prepared to push her away when the heavy metal door popped open once more, letting the raucous party music trickle out.

"*Amore?*"

Shame curdled my stomach. Or maybe that was the vodka. With lust-fuzzy vision, I saw Sergio standing to our right, hands on his hips. The sides of his gray suit jacket pulled back to expose his lean torso and his crisp white shirt covered the muscles I knew by touch.

Tears burned the rims of my eyes as I waited for his anger, his jealousy. As open-minded as he was, Sergio was also deliciously possessive. His hand shot out and I grasped it like a lifeline. He pulled me against his body. The door slammed closed behind him. While I shivered, I watched Trina blanch.

"I thought...shit." Her fingers clenched on empty air. The hollow laugh that followed almost made me want to hug her.

"Add that to the list of apologies." She turned to go, her bony shoulders hunched under the thin sky-blue sweater she wore.

"Ekaterina, wait." Sergio's deep, lyrical voice startled us both. He left my side and Trina's eyes widened as he walked to her, arm outstretched. "Have lunch with us tomorrow." We both gaped at him, but Trina moved before I did, snatching at the business card he offered.

"Why?" Her voice was strained, her eyes watery.

An elegant shrug was her reply. "You are important to my Katie."

She transferred her attention to me. "*Kotonok?*" The hope in her voice tightened my throat until I could only nod in reply. With three deep breaths, I reminded myself how deeply I trusted Sergio. I could follow his lead. Maybe this would offer some kind of cathartic resolution with Trina, considering our last words to each other had been ugly and cruel.

Like that had buoyed her, Trina stood tall and looked at the card. "I have rehearsal all day. Could we do dinner? I can take a cab over."

"Is the orchestra visiting New York?" The question was out of my mouth before I could think twice.

She ignored me, instead waiting for Sergio's answer. "Of course, *bella*. Does six work?"

Trina nodded, then turned to go. "I'm with the New York Philharmonic now," she tossed out before retreating into the night.

We made sweet, frantic love that night after Sergio reassured me he wasn't angry. No, he understood.

"You still want her, *amore*. I see why." Staccato thrusts pierced his statement. "I would be so hard, watching you together. Watching you kiss her. Watching you make love. Tasting you on her lips."

I had come so hard stars danced behind my eyes. Until tonight, it had all been pretend, keeping things exciting in the bedroom. Now it was real. Possibilities ringed rosy in my dreams until I woke, chest tight with anxious hope.

The whole day I struggled to focus on my work. The only highlight was grabbing a quick lunch with Sergio—there were benefits to working in the same building, even if we were floors apart. Normally, our quick lunch bolstered me through the day, but today's was fraught with tense undertones. Regardless, I loved knowing he was nearby, especially when tensions in Africa had our whole political affairs office in a frenzy.

It seemed like I'd be able to escape on time, until a last-minute emergency crossed my inbox right before 6:00 p.m. Damn, I hated being late. Especially since I'd wanted a couple minutes alone with Sergio.

No dice. When I stepped off the elevator at 6:12, his laughter caught my attention, quickly followed by a familiar giggle.

They hadn't caught sight of me, so I paused to watch my past and present lovers sitting next to each other on a couch in the lobby with their shoulders turned inward so they were almost facing each other.

I waited for the pang of jealousy that usually gripped me when a beautiful woman set her sights on Sergio, but none came. They looked good together. Relaxed, natural. Instead of what I used to call her "plastic public smirk," the guise Trina donned when performing on stage, she graced him with her true smile.

They both caught sight of me at the same time and my body burned with need as I walked to them. Sergio ducked his head and whispered into Trina's ear. Two hungry looks were leveled on me. I had never felt sexier in my life.

Damn, he worked fast. To be fair, it had been the same with him and me.

My panties fucking melted along with coherence. "Hi."

Lame. Well done, Katie. I capped it off with a little wave, even though they were both within touching distance.

Sergio pulled me into a hug, planted a kiss on my forehead, then gestured to the door. I wanted a kiss from Trina, too.

Walking the blocks between the office and one of our favorite dive restaurants did nothing to dissipate the building need in me. The little Mediterranean diner, run by three generations of a Lebanese family, had become an easy default meal when neither Sergio nor I felt like cooking. As a bonus, it was dimly lit and crowded, which provided a sense of privacy.

Sergio gestured for me to take the inside of the booth, then maneuvered Ekaterina to follow. She scooted closer than was strictly necessary while he took the seat opposite me.

Aban, the owner's grandson, took our order, which Sergio rattled off: Massaya Classic wine and batata harra to start, followed by kofta kebabs and the delicious vegetarian stew with rice, bazella.

"I'll have the kofta kebabs too," Trina added.

"Really?" I looked at her out of the corner of my eye. She'd been a painfully picky eater in college, sticking with bland basics. "That's lamb, you know."

I caught her rolling her eyes, then she elbowed me. "Ten years is a long time."

Understatement of the year.

Sergio pulled us back from the lull in conversation and soon we were all chatting and laughing like three old friends, filling in the gaps of the past decade. She might have become a more adventurous eater, but Trina was the same bubbly, flirtatious bitch I'd fallen in love with. She scooted closer under the guise of getting to the batata harra, until her slim hip cozied up to my rounder one. She didn't move even when the entrees were set down. My right side tingled from her body heat.

We'd had enough wine that my defenses were down, and I

had seen Ekaterina's drunk-lazy smile enough through the meal to know she was probably buzzed too. While the conversation flowed and I heard tales of her time in Saint Petersburg's famous orchestra, Trina's hand settled on my thigh. I jumped, and got a popped eyebrow from Sergio. My skin flushed—he *knew*.

Sergio maintained the dialogue while I closed my eyes and imagined her fingerprints searing into my skin so she would always be with me.

"You are beautiful, *kotonok*. Soft." Trina ran a finger up my thigh. "I want to touch you everywhere."

I gasped and tensed in the seat. Sergio leaned across the table until it seemed the world was just us three. "I had an enlightening conversation with the lovely Ekaterina while we waited for you."

She picked up the thread of conversation. "I didn't believe you'd missed me. Sergio let me know he had been helping you remember our time together."

In the dim corner where we sat, her fingers skimmed across the swell of my breast beneath my staid green cardigan and cream silk shell. Scrabbling for a defense against her witchy touch, I said, "You can't leave like you did and pick things up a fucking decade later!"

Trina turned to Sergio. "Still has a dirty mouth, hmm?"

He smirked. "Dirtier."

"Good," she whispered in my ear. "I love hearing you talk dirty. And I want to apologize. Profusely. With my lips." She nipped my earlobe and goose bumps exploded down my back. "And my fingers and tongue."

Lord, I was outnumbered. Hopelessly outmaneuvered. And to be honest...I didn't want to fight. Why punish myself with more wet dreams, when I could have Trina, in the flesh, one more time?

"Yes," I said.

* * *

I don't remember paying the bill or hopping in a cab or traveling across the bridge to the luxurious two-bedroom condo Sergio and I had purchased last year. Aside from Trina's hands wandering my body, nothing hit my radar. And since this was New York, no one cared about a threesome snuggling in the back of a cab.

Pressed between their bodies, I reclined against Sergio's reassuring strength while Trina teased. Finally we arrived and poured from the cab, drunk on lust and wine.

We stumbled up four flights of stairs to the top condo. As soon as Sergio unlocked the door, we burst through in a fit of flying clothing and grasping hands. I had peripheral awareness of him moving away to recline on the couch with a small glass of Vin Santo.

Then Trina's lips found mine and her almost-nude body pressed into my curves and everything winked out of existence. She traced the same paths Sergio would, but the rough calluses on the tips of her left-hand fingers hit nerves his work-soft hands didn't, from neck to the V between my breasts to the round swell of my stomach to the dip of my waist. Trina clung to the soft flesh of my hips and thrust her knee between my legs.

"I can feel how hot you are. God, I missed this." Traces of her Russian accent, vestiges of a childhood immigration, lurked in her voice when she was truly aroused. She whispered to me in her native tongue and my stomach flip-flopped at her fluency.

"Picked up more than good eating habits, huh?"

Redundant question. She answered with a deep kiss that left me gasping for Trina-scented air.

A shove to my shoulder, then I was falling back, caught in Sergio's strong arms. "Hold on, *amore*." His thighs spread my own and, like a dream, Trina knelt between them and made good on her promise.

I lost count of how many times she brought me to the edge before backing off, but after each one she kissed me and said, "I'm sorry, *dorogaya*." Her endearment—*darling*—struck my heart.

Then, "Forgive me, *lyubov moya*." She chipped away with the next volley—*my love*.

After I'd lost count of her teasing near-orgasms, she laved my aching nipples and pleaded. "*Ty nuzhna mnye.*" *I need you* broke down my walls.

Next time I writhed in pleasure, my knees quaking around her ears, she kissed me and whispered, "*Ya ne mogu zhit' bez tebya.*" *I can't live without you.*

Ah, god. I caved. It's not like I had healed after she left; no, that wound was still open and raw because a piece of me had been missing. And if I wanted us to have a shot at any kind of relationship—even friends, since she'd been my best—grudges and resentment and regret had to get the boot. I pulled out the one sentence of Russian I remembered. After all, I'd whispered it into the ether every day. "*Ya tozhe tebya lyublyu.*" *I love you too.*

This time, she let me come, her fingers deep inside me and lips swallowing my cries.

From behind me, Sergio shifted. His erection nudging into my back presented a stark reminder of our mixed company. For an ugly moment, I resented him. I'd had my Trina back, all to myself...but that had never been the deal.

Then the moment twisted and Trina kissed him, her lips glossy with my flavor. Jealousy burned away. I whimpered, pressed between their hot, hard bodies, so different from my own.

Neither let me wallow with those dark thoughts. No, their hands, as if choreographed, roamed my body while their tongues made love. I was included, even while on the periphery. Their fingers entered me at the same time and I shook between them.

"Bedroom." Sergio's voice cracked through the air.

My mind calculated all the ways the three of us could combine, leaving me to follow mutely behind their sinuous forms. They were almost the same height, my bookend lovers—one as pale and ethereal as the other was dark and commanding.

Sergio wended his hand in Trina's hair and hauled her against him for a feral kiss. "Unzip me."

Her pupils were so dilated her eyes looked like the deep, endless middle of the ocean. I drowned in them while she stripped Sergio. We didn't break eye contact until he was as naked as we were, and only then because he grabbed her arm, spun her to face the bed, and pushed her onto it.

Even from halfway across the room, I could see the shine of wetness on her pussy. She'd always loved it rough; one thing I had never quite been able to offer. Satisfaction slowed my racing heart.

"Lie on the bed, *amore*. You are going to lick her until she comes, then until I tell you to stop."

While I rushed to comply, I heard the now-unfamiliar crinkle and rip of a condom. *He'd planned for this eventuality.*

My friends would have balked, called him a dog. A letch. An opportunist.

I thanked god I found him. Thoughtful, loving, understanding.

And yes...a man who was a wonderful opportunist.

Once I was in position, Trina climbed fully onto the bed, curling over my body to make up for the difference in our heights. I gripped her strong thighs and arched up until my tongue met the clit peeking eagerly out from its hood. She squealed against my touch and bit my hip. I sucked the nub, remembering exactly how she liked to be touched. My thumbs spread her pussy lips and I licked into her, a teasing prelude to the impending penetration. Arching my head back, I saw Sergio at the edge of the bed, waiting. His cock was still, veins throbbing with the surge of blood. I knew if I took him in my mouth, he'd barely fit. I loved when he was this turned on.

I backed off when he stepped closer, positioning himself at her entrance. Enthralled, captivated, I stared as he nudged the head inside.

He cursed. "You are so tight."

My stomach fluttered. I wanted to finger her, feel the walls of her cunt squeeze around me. In solace, I licked her clit again and continued up to Sergio's waiting shaft. They both shuddered, and his cock slipped farther inside her.

Trina's muffled voice reached me. "It's been awhile."

Later, when I held her against my breast and combed my fingers through her hair, I'd make her tell me exactly how long. I'd forgotten how much I missed falling asleep like that. Now that it was within reach, I wanted to seize it with both hands.

"Please, please. I need—"

He surged inside her and she cried out. I watched her flutter around him and knew her body was adjusting to his girth. I licked around their joining, sucking at her clit and soothing until her hips canted back, begging for more.

"You must stay very still, *bella*. Just like this, so Katie can tongue that pretty pussy."

She whimpered and her hot breath blew against my splayed legs. I'd need them both again, soon. Heat built in my core as I pleasured her in time to Sergio's slow thrusts.

As we found our rhythm and his hips pistoned into her, I brought her to orgasm once, then again, before Sergio succumbed to her clinging pussy.

Sweaty, exhausted, and just barely sated, I turned on the bed and pulled Trina into my arms. By the time Sergio returned from cleaning up, we were a tangle of limbs in the middle of the mattress.

Undeterred, he crawled in behind me to spoon against my back.

This was bliss.

Until that ugly little voice crept in. Their arms both tensed. Sergio asked the building question. "What is wrong, *amore*?"

I sighed, resigned to hashing this out. Neither would allow my thoughts to fester for long. They were too clever by half—and here I was, voluntarily putting myself between their all-too-capable hands. "What now?" Even though I knew the answer, felt the inevitability of *us*, as truly as I knew I loved them both, I had to hear it.

Trina laughed, the purr rumbling through my chest. "I have two guest tickets for Wednesday's performance. The concert is at seven, but I hope you don't have plans later that night. There's this quiet hallway, see, with an old, abandoned dressing room..."

SUNSHINE

Emerald

Her dark hair hung long and straight past her shoulders, almost covering one eye as she spoke to the bartender. She didn't smile, but neither did she look grim as she faced forward and waited for her drink.

Sean sidled over to her. Up close, her features were striking, set in smooth pale skin surrounding dark-brown eyes. She met his gaze in the mirror behind the bar without turning to him, and he smiled.

"Hi," he said easily. "I'm Sean." He held out his hand.

She faced him at last, looking in his eyes for a beat before shaking his hand. "Kelly." She wore little makeup, and the edge of a tattoo peeked out above the top button of her blouse. He smiled wryly when she caught him looking.

"I'm sorry. I was just noticing your tattoo."

She nodded and casually hooked her fingers over the edge of the lavender fabric, pulling it to the side so he could see the tattoo fully. It was positioned high enough above her left breast that showing it was not inappropriate.

The design was a round clock face, intricate with its twelve Roman numerals and solid black hands positioned at just after seven o'clock. Sean studied the precise numerals and tiny black indicators between each one, struck by their meticulous resemblance to those of a genuine clock. Each hand blossomed from its respective black arm into an elaborate tangle of swirls and then back to a pristine point. The ink around the border gave the impression of a shiny casing, and the entire thing was about the size of a silver dollar.

"Interesting," he said, his curiosity piqued. "I've never encountered a clock tattoo before. What made you choose it?"

She was watching him steadily. "It's the time my daughter died. 7:02. My way of showing her I'll never forget her."

Startled by the revelation, Sean took an involuntary step back, then immediately regretted it. Kelly smiled a tight, tiny smile and turned to accept her drink as the bartender brought it to her. Sean put a hand up when she got out her purse and ordered one for himself, pulling cash from his wallet and handing it to the bartender. Kelly had paused, and for a moment he thought she would argue, but then she lowered her hands and nodded his way.

"Thank you."

Her voice, like her expression, was neutral. She had not yet seemed unwelcoming, but Sean found himself more unsure than usual whether his presence was desired. His gaze flicked up to the mirror behind the bar again, where he watched her surreptitiously as she looked away from him toward the sun blazing in through the wide window. The lobby doors behind them were swishing steadily, hotel patrons leaving for the day or bustling to check-in. Sean detected a trace of weariness in Kelly's face that was more than momentary, as though it had been etched in over time. There was something familiar about her as well.

"When did she die?" Had it been recently? Her daughter

must have been very young, as Kelly couldn't be older than thirty, though people sometimes thought that about him, and he had turned thirty-two earlier in the year.

"Two years ago."

"I'm sorry." The words sounded pathetically inadequate, but he wasn't about to not say them. They might not be sufficient, but they were true.

Was she married? Sean looked and didn't see a ring on any of her fingers. Her short, unpainted nails looked delicate somehow, contrasting with the rest of her appearance and everything else he'd seen about her thus far.

As she faced forward again and took a drink, Sean felt at a sudden loss. He didn't know how to comfort her or if that was what she was even looking for. Feeling a wave of defeat, he opened his mouth to excuse himself. At best, it seemed he was in her way; at worst, he was presenting an unwelcome nuisance.

Before he could speak, she said, "Don't go."

"What?"

She glanced at him, then turned back to her drink. "I know you're about to leave. I don't want you to."

He stared at her. She looked back at him. "I'm not very good at talking to people. It's taken me a while to learn that I give the impression that I don't want them around. Sometimes that's true, but not always." Her eyes flicked to the ground, then to the row of liquors lining the mirror behind the bar. "It's not true now."

Sean blinked. He wasn't sure he had ever met someone so simultaneously enigmatic and direct. Being around her was putting him through paces he was unused to: in a span of twenty minutes, he'd felt attraction, curiosity, sympathy, awkwardness, defeat, and something like poignancy. Was whatever was going on in this encounter worth what might come out of it?

Even as the question arose in him, Sean was aware he

couldn't know the answer. He was surprised to realize it didn't feel as important to him as he expected.

"Well, I—"

She interrupted him by standing up and kissing him. It shocked him more than anything she'd done so far, and she was already pulling away by the time his arms reached around her waist. She turned, leaving him more baffled than ever as she sat back on her stool.

Unsure what to say, Sean angled his body back toward the bar as well and took a drink. He met her eyes again in the mirror, and this time she held his gaze. Her blouse sat such that her tattoo was about half visible now, and her hands were gathered around the glass in front of her.

He shifted a bit. The suddenness and unexpected intensity of her kiss had caused his cock to harden, and the smell of her hair that now lingered in his memory wasn't helping.

Kelly slid off her seat toward him. Sean backed up to give her room, and she looked up at him.

"What do you want?" she asked.

He blanched. What was he supposed to say? As he started fumbling for an answer, the question struck him: what *did* he want?

"I mean, there must have been a reason you came over to talk to me," she continued. "What was it?"

Emboldened by her straightforwardness, Sean went with the truth. "I found you attractive."

"And do you still?"

Sean was waiting to see some form of expression in her face. The neutrality, especially in contrast to that kiss, was a bit unnerving.

"Yes."

Her mask slipped then, and he sucked in a breath at the sudden and unequivocal softness he saw. The placidity moved back into place quickly enough, but that moment was like the crack in an invisible door letting through a tiny beam of purest sunshine. And suddenly what Sean wanted more than anything else right then was to see it come out again.

"Come upstairs with me," he murmured. Not a demand. A request. Perhaps even a plea.

He allowed himself to hope that her falling into step beside him was an acceptance. His hand hovered over the small of Kelly's back as she walked with him to the elevator, and by the time they stepped into it, Sean wanted to push her to the floor and cover her body with his. He flushed, feeling inappropriate at the primitive musing. He glanced over and found her staring at him. Kelly's eyes seemed to have deepened somehow, and for a second he thought he saw the same urge reflected in them. He looked away, working to convince himself he was mistaken before he made an ass of himself.

Seconds later they walked side by side to the room he had checked into only a couple of hours before. Sean opened the door and reached for the light, then turned when he felt her hand cover his before he could flip the switch.

"Leave it off," she whispered.

When they emerged from the entryway, he saw that the natural light spilling through the half-open curtains made the lights superfluous anyway. He turned to Kelly, and before he could say anything, she was kissing him again, pressing against him this time with an urgency that, though understated, was unmistakable. He reached for the buttons of her blouse as she backed onto the bed and pulled him on top of her.

Kelly reached up and undid the front clasp of her bra as her blouse fell open. Her tattoo looked sedately out from her chest, and without meaning to, Sean reached and brushed over it with his thumb, registering a strange tightening in his heart as it reappeared from beneath his skin. His hand slid down and caressed the breast below her tattoo with a reverence that surprised him, and as he replaced the fingers that skimmed over her nipple with his lips, his touch was more delicate than he'd known it could be.

Kelly's chest surged with her inhale, and he heard her breath hitch as his tongue slid over her skin. Then she spoke.

"You don't have to be gentle with me."

He pulled away at the directive, both startled and yet not surprised by it. He realized he had been being gentle, not because he wanted to but because he felt like he should for some reason. An uncertainty that was becoming familiar filled him, and he paused.

Kelly slid out from underneath him and rolled him over. Straddling him, she sat up and let her shirt fall the rest of the way off. Sean's erection was straining against his jeans even as he felt a lingering trepidation. Kelly held his gaze, and he found he had trouble meeting her eyes. He felt somehow wrong for wanting her, as though she had enough to deal with without some lecherous bullshit from him.

"If you want me," she said, the look in her eyes now demanding that he meet them, "I'm right here." Her voice dropped to a whisper. "Take me."

It was as though the words reached through and pulled whatever was blocking him inside right out of him. Sean grabbed her hips, and her breath expelled as he ground himself up against her before lifting her so he could pop his jeans open. She backed off to give him room, and he almost came as she licked her lips, staring down at his cock as it sprang from his open zipper. He gritted his teeth against the urge to shove her head down onto it. He was desperate to be inside her—any part of her. Kelly sent him a sidelong glance filled with an unnerving knowingness.

"What did I tell you?" she asked.

"What do you mean?" He was having trouble breathing

through the pulsing in his cock, which was demanding attention with little room for intellect.

"I said you don't have to be gentle with me." Still kneeling next to his waist, she shifted so she was facing him. "You want to slam my mouth down on your cock." She said it as though this was undisputed, and Sean sucked in a breath. "You are, for some reason, resisting doing that," she continued. "Why?"

Sean thought his whole body might burst from the combination of resistance and frustration. He felt about as much like carrying on a conversation right then as he did hiking up Mount Everest.

"I don't know," he burst out.

Kelly didn't smile. Shrugging, she said, "Have it your way, then. Put your hands behind your head." He did as she said. "Keep them there. But know that what I wanted was for you to grab my hair with both hands and fuck my throat."

Her words made his cock almost hurt, and he couldn't hold back the sharp moan that escaped him. Kelly reached out and ran her fingers lightly up his hard length, and Sean thought he might cry. When she looked at him again, a smile played around her lips.

The next instant her warm mouth was covering him, taking him to the back of her throat, and he clenched his teeth and did everything he could not to come. Kelly arched her back, stretching her lithe body and lifting one leg over him so her pussy came to rest right above his face. As though the energy of not climaxing was shooting a fire right back up his core, Sean yanked his hands out from under his head and seized her hips, covering her velvety folds with his mouth. He took a breath and somehow amassed the precision to tap his tongue against her clit even as her moans against his cock made him feel he might explode. He shuddered beneath her for another few seconds before bucking up into her with a yell, unable to hold back anymore as he emptied himself into her mouth.

Kelly swung around and rose to her knees, and before he could even ask, she did as he was about to direct and straddled his face. Sean's tongue found its way back to her clit like a magnet, his full concentration now on bringing out of her what she had just released in him. Kelly gyrated against him, beginning to whimper, and reached and grasped his hair. It was in her hands that he felt the combination of vulnerability and abandon that made him look up, let his concentration slip just enough so that he could see her face, eyes closed, features wreathed with an expression that was somehow hopelessly far away and immediate all at once. Whatever it was, it wasn't a mask this time.

She tugged his hair, a silent urging, and he knew she knew he had stopped to look at her. He returned with vigor to the single-minded desire to make her come. Make her surrender. Make her fly.

And come she did. Seconds, or perhaps minutes—it all became the same—later, her body began to tremble, and he could feel the moment when she lost control and thrashed against him like a flag whipping in the wind, a beautiful, strangled cry wrenching from her throat. Sean held her hips to keep her steady, holding his tongue in place until her undulations stopped and she seemed to deflate, her sweat-covered body sliding down his until she landed with her head on his shoulder, more as though by accident than by design. He rested his hands on the warmth of her back and listened to her breathing until it evened.

"You still don't know me, do you?"

Sean blinked. He wasn't sure how many minutes had passed; it was possible he'd fallen asleep as they'd lain there. Kelly had lifted her head and shifted slightly so she wasn't on him anymore but rather lay on her stomach beside him. He stared at her.

"I beg your pardon?"

She smiled softly. "That would be a no." He was relieved to see she didn't seem offended by this even as he racked his brain for a recollection of when he might have met her.

She spoke again after a few moments.

"You were at the retirement party for Benjamin Marcus three summers ago at Cobbs Park." She didn't state it as a question, but when she paused, Sean confirmed.

"Yeah, I worked at his company right out of college. He wasn't the CEO yet then, and I worked with him personally on a fairly regular basis."

"My husband at the time had worked at his company a couple years before, and I met you in passing near the fountain. You talked about the fountains you'd just seen in Paris." Kelly ran a hand through her dark hair and flipped it over her shoulder. "I thought that might have been why you spoke to me downstairs. I thought maybe you recognized me."

Sean almost winced in embarrassment. Not only had he not remembered her, he had just managed to engage in quite intimate contact with her and still not realized they had met before. Of course, now that she'd reminded him, he couldn't believe he hadn't recognized her. He recalled their conversation clearly, how she'd said she hadn't been to Paris but hoped to go someday. He wondered if she had yet.

"You changed your hair color," he blurted.

"Yes, I was blonde then."

A recollection accosted him with a sickening jolt. He didn't speak it out loud. She'd had a little girl with her that day, a high-energy presence with a popsicle and long blonde pigtails hurtling around the fountain and surrounding grass.

Kelly was watching him, and though he didn't know how, Sean was sure she knew what he had just remembered. Averting his eyes, he found them automatically drawn to the tattoo above her left breast. The intricacy of the hands really was striking.

"You don't have to feel sorry whenever you look at it." He started at her voice, but there was no harshness in her tone. There wasn't even reprimand. "It's not a symbol of sorrow. It's a symbol of love."

Somehow he hadn't expected to hear something so seemingly sentimental come out of her mouth. He looked up at her, and her eyes instantly told him there was nothing sentimental about it. He had never associated love with such stoic equanimity, and once again his experience of her seemed to fly in the face of basic notions he hadn't even realized he rarely questioned.

"So. You...aren't married anymore?"

"I'm not."

"Why are you here at this hotel?" Sean suddenly realized how odd it was that two local people would encounter each other at a hotel bar. "Don't you live here anymore?" A tiny stab of consternation zipped through him as he said it.

She shook her head. "I moved about an hour and a half away from here. My sister just graduated from grad school, and I came back yesterday for the ceremony and her party. I didn't feel like making the drive afterward, so I stayed here for the night."

An hour and a half. That's not so bad. Sean was startled to find the thought in his consciousness. Refocusing, he wondered why she hadn't just stayed at her sister's, but something held him back from asking as he glanced at her.

"What about you? Or do you make a habit of hanging out at local hotel bars to talk to women you find attractive?" Her smirk was overt.

Sean flushed and hoped she didn't notice. The idea wasn't unheard of for him. He was glad that in this case he had a legitimate excuse. "My company's holding a conference here for the next few days. I'll need to be up early tomorrow to start setting up, so it was easier to just stay here for the night. I was just in the bar to grab something to eat before some last-minute prep work. I had just finished and was on my way out when I saw you."

Kelly nodded in acknowledgment and flipped onto her back. She stretched, her breasts thrusting upward with the arch of her pale back, and Sean shifted as his cock hardened again.

"Well, I suppose I'd better get going," she said when her body relaxed, turning back onto her side toward him.

"Why?" The question slipped from Sean's mouth before he could stop it.

Kelly's dark eyes turned to him, their neutral gaze now familiar. She paused an extra second before she said, "Why not?"

Sean detected more than a casual flippancy in her question. He looked into her eyes, searching for the light he'd seen in the bar. He was only slightly surprised to recognize that the urge that enveloped him again to entice it out of her went beyond the insistent tingling in his cock.

He remembered her earlier admonition that he didn't have to be gentle with her. Without warning, he pinned her beneath him as his lips pushed against hers. The tiny shriek that escaped her, half arousal and half surprise, made his cock surge with the desire to be inside her. She pushed up against him, then pulled her lips from his.

"We need a condom," she whispered.

Sean caught her gaze, and he nodded. "Of course." He gave her a quick kiss before pushing himself up. "One second." He fumbled in his small suitcase for the box of condoms he had brought with him, flushing again as he hoped she didn't ask if he brought condoms with him to all the conferences he attended. He did.

As he ripped one open, she held out her hand. He stepped forward and handed it to her, watching as she pulled the wrapper off and rolled onto her stomach so she was sideways on the bed. She gestured for him to come closer, and he did, stopping with his knees touching the bedspread in front of her. With a sly glance up at him, Kelly slipped the condom into her mouth and rose up on her elbows. Positioning herself directly above him, she opened her lips and slid them down his cock.

Sean's mouth fell open a little. When she pulled back, she smoothed the condom the rest of the way down with one hand and flipped back over.

"That's something you don't see every day," he breathed.

That elicited a little smile from the stunning woman on the bed, and Sean grinned back as he climbed on top of her, sliding his sheathed cock against her clit for a few seconds until her breath hitched. Then he sank into her, gritting his teeth to keep from coming again as her heat enveloped him. Kelly's legs slid around his thighs, and Sean started to thrust slowly, knowing he would come if he moved faster.

When she pushed against him, he acquiesced and rolled over. Kelly sat atop him, keeping his slow pace at first; as he covered her clit with his thumb, however, she bit her lip and was soon bouncing on his cock like an exercise ball, her breath quickening as he sensed her nearing climax. Seconds later she squealed and fell forward to grab his chest, riding him in a frenzy as the orgasm swept through her.

As it had been the first time, watching her state of abandon was breathtaking. Sean's release burst through any attempt to corral it just as Kelly's subsided. Her body draped across his chest as he gripped her hips, burying his cock to the hilt as it pulsed inside her.

Sean watched as she got dressed.

"Is there anything you need to get home for right away?" he asked suddenly.

Her face impassive, Kelly answered, "No," after a tiny hesitation.

"Would you stay here with me? Tonight?" He felt a tightness inside at the idea of her leaving. "I mean, I have to get up really early in the morning, but..." His voice trailed off. "I suppose you have to work tomorrow, too, though, and don't want to have to drive an hour and a half to get there." Something inside him deflated even as he said it.

"I'm off tomorrow. I'm a nurse. I don't go back to work until Tuesday afternoon."

Sean's heart jumped a little. "Really? Well, if you wanted, you could stay here tomorrow night, too. I'll be busy all day, but I'll be done by early evening." He looked down, suddenly embarrassed by his eagerness. She probably had things to do, and here he was asking her to sit around in an empty hotel room all day waiting for him. "I'm sorry. I guess you wouldn't want to spend all day here by yourself."

"I'm pretty sure I could find ways to entertain myself," Kelly said dryly. "And quite frankly, I like to be by myself."

Sean looked up. Kelly's intent gaze was on him, and the corners of her mouth turned up in a little smile. "But not always." She stood up.

"Yes, I will stay with you tonight." The smile still gracing her lips belied the formality of the delivery, and he grinned up at her. Spontaneously she let out a giggle, and Sean caught his breath as the sunshine burst through again for the first time since they'd been in the bar. She composed herself quickly, but the brilliance of what he'd seen twice now wasn't so easily forgotten. In fact, he wasn't sure he ever would.

"I checked my bag in at the front desk when I decided to hang out in the bar for a while," she said. "I'll go down and get it."

Sean walked her to the door, resisting the urge to grab her and drag her back to bed as she reached for the handle. There would be time. More time than just the next two nights if he had anything to do with it.

He watched from the doorway as she headed down the hall toward the elevator. Her gait was reserved, but it didn't concern him. She had her reasons for the reserve and the impassiveness and the weariness, he knew. But it was the light they covered up that most interested—mesmerized, if he was honest with himself—him now. Sean stepped back into the room and let the door drift shut behind him, ready to spend his foreseeable future doing everything he could to help it shine.

HOW TO GET YOUR WIFE BACK, IN ONLY ABOUT A MILLION STEPS

Claire de Winter

I dial my brother from the office before I leave. No one at home is waiting for me. I light a cigarette. Yeah, it's against the rules, but I excel at meaningless acts of bravado. No smoking allowed in the office, no smoking in the entire building and a three-foot radius around it. Elise hates it when she smells smoke on me. I listen to the phone ringing down the line, wondering if Scott will pick up in Oregon.

On the outside everything is a sweet ideal, everything I've worked for, really. My brother, though, knows better.

Scott picks up on the tenth ring; he once said voice mail was for fascists.

"We've just lost touch," I say into the phone without preamble. "I can't get her back."

"Dude…" If there's one thing about Scott, it's his ability to pick up right where you are. It's a rare gift to find an ally in one's own family, I'm aware. "You guys have tiny kids. She doesn't want out. She wants a nap."

"That's part of the problem," I say, and yes, I know I'm the jerk here. My wife has twins. *We* have twins.

"You just need some spice. Unless someone's humiliating someone on a daily basis, is there something you're not telling me?"

"Ha fucking ha," I say, knowing he's both jokingly referring to kink, but also seriously asking on a different level.

"What you need is to go to Vegas, check into a hotel, smoke a joint and see where it leads. We've discussed the benefits of hotel sex."

That's my bro. Almost any of his problems can be solved by checking out of the world and into hedonism. Leaving the babies for the weekend wasn't going to work for Elise, or me, or the twins for that matter.

"Don't make me come back there and knock some sense into your head," Scott is saying. "You're never going to do better than Elise. You know that, right?"

And I have to admit, I agree. Scott's always liked Elise. Not in a creepy way; Scott doesn't go for the Elise type. He prefers them small and dark and troubled. But I know he thinks she's better than I deserve, which is a compliment in its own weird way. He's both wiser than his years and has no problem calling me out.

"Because that's what I've learned." I can hear Scott's lighter click in the background, can hear him holding in the smoke as he says, "You can kill it, man. Love is something to guard."

My house is dark and sleeping when I get home, though it's only nine o'clock. Elise acts on the advice that one should sleep when the babies sleep. They'd all just started sleeping through the night. I tell myself she goes to bed early to make up for the insane sleep deficit from the last months. I tell myself it won't always be like this.

I pour a bourbon, neat, and sit in my dark living room because, the truth is, I miss my wife.

I think about waking her, about light touches and kisses until she's overcome with lust. I've tried a few times, but she's sleepily brushed me off and rolled over, and I have to admit that crushes the ego a little. Rationality and babies and sleep deprivation be damned, a guy still wants to be wanted, even by his wife, *especially* by his wife. I've pulled all the enticing moves I can think of and wound up feeling like a pervert trying to fuck a sleeping person or a jerk demanding sex from a new mother.

And I don't want to be one more demand. She has enough new demands on her already. I check my needs and myself regularly, daily—hourly, it feels like. I'm becoming nervous that this is never going to stop, that this is the new reality of our lives with kids. At this point I feel like if she gives in to me, I'll be so relieved I'll never stop asking for more, never stop taking. And where would that leave us?

I down my drink and soon I'm lost, like I often am lately, thinking of the day we got married. The day we started down this whole path, I guess. The day I had finally locked her in, because yeah, I won't lie, that's how I think of it. There was no way in hell I was letting this woman get away. She'd just broken up with her ex, the idiot. And I went right after her, as her type doesn't come on the market very often—rarely single for long, men "friends" always hovering around waiting for a chance. I had rushed her, but she'd said yes.

And the honeymoon; I lean my head back. My girl doesn't do beaches—too pale and she hates bathing suits. What is it with women and that shit anyway? "My tits are too big. I have this thing here," she says, pointing. Women are insane sometimes if you ask me. As if tits can be too big, and pointing at some insignificant nothing. She looks like creamy, pale heaven with a smattering of freckles in a bathing suit. Anyway, we went to Paris, instead, for a week of eating and fucking. She bought all this incredibly complicated lacy stuff that the French are famous for. It was great.

And just thinking about it, about the way her face looked... I'd never felt more wanted, more desired, I guess. I unzip my pants and pull myself out. I can't help it; I'm already hard. It doesn't take much these days. I stroke up once and then down. Yeah, I'm in my living room spanking it to thoughts of my wife who's sleeping upstairs. I feel sad and pathetic and yet, I'm not going to stop. I want release. I want to feel good. But mostly, I just want her. And when I come, it's to thoughts of her under me, in that huge white Paris bed, whispering dirty things in my ear that are all about how much she needs me, wants me—like this.

After I've finished, I realize this has not been my most thought-through adventure as I'm left with a mess in my hand, in my lap, probably on my pants. I get myself situated as best I can and head upstairs.

The room is dark and I don't turn on the light. I can make her out—a small hillock under the covers. I strip in the dark, and get in the shower, hoping not to wake her.

I drop the soap when the lights come on. She's standing there, one hand over her eyebrows, shielding her eyes from the harsh bathroom glare. She's in that old-fashioned nightgown she doesn't know I like. White cotton to the floor with lace and shit, like a granny gown, but it's so old and worn that it's practically see-through to all the curviness underneath, a perfect mix of innocence and decadence.

"Hey." I pop my head out the shower door. "I didn't mean to wake you." Though I'm secretly glad to see her.

"You're showering?" she asks. "You never shower at night."

I'm soaping my head. "Yeah, long day. I feel grimy."

"You've been smoking," she guesses, picking up my clothes.

I'm already turning off the water and wrapping a towel around my waist when she holds out my boxers. "What is this?"

I'm not squeamish about discussing masturbation. Everyone does it right? Including her; she's no prude. But I'm instantly embarrassed like I'm thirteen and my mom has caught me.

"Nothing," I say, swiping the boxers out of her hand and stuffing them in the hamper. "You know what it is."

"Nothing?" she asks, and I recognize the edge of panic in her voice. "Are you having an affair?" Tears are welling in her eyes.

"Jesus," I say, exasperated because I really don't want to admit I was jerking it downstairs to thoughts of her, and I'm just a pathetic lovesick loser who misses her. I doubt she'd believe it anyway. I'm a grown man, a father now, and I'm allowed my privacy. Right? "No."

"You come home with jizz on your pants and you're not having an affair? Were you at a strip club?"

This kind of makes me laugh, it's so off base. My girl has no idea what happens at strip clubs. Plus that's not my scene. I mean, no judgment on guys who dig getting grinded on by naked chicks. I can understand the appeal. And I've been to bachelor parties. But that's never been my thing—variety. I'm more into intensity.

"I was downstairs in the living room."

"Watching porn?"

Okay, I take a peek every once in a while. She knows this.

"No, not watching porn. Jacking off."

"I'm supposed to believe you came home to jack off in the living room by yourself without porn?" she says with exaggerated disbelief. "Why didn't you wake me?"

I put my arms around her even though I'm still wet. "You're tired. You need your sleep." See what I did there? Scoring points. Plus it's the truth.

She kind of sniffles in my chest a little bit, and then she says the craziest thing she's ever said to me.

"You don't want me anymore."

"The hell I don't."

"I've heard of this. Husbands who have affairs when the babies are little. I just...I didn't think..."

"I'm not having an affair." I'm keeping calm, reminding myself she's tired. "How can you even say that to me?"

"You come home with...or you didn't come get me. Either way..."

"I fucking adore you."

"But you're not attracted to me anymore."

"I'm trying not to be a dick. You're exhausted. We have twins for god's sake."

"That stretched out my stomach..."

"Not this again." I run my hands up and down her back.

"Is this because you watched the birth?" She's asked this before. Can't lie, the birth was bloodier than I ever imagined, but also fascinating. I took tons of pictures, which pissed her off. The doc said I was less squeamish than most dads he had seen. What can I say? I can hang.

But I know she's read articles or talked to her girls about how watching the birth can put a man off sex.

"The births were a total miracle." See how I go for the points again?

This, at least, makes her smile because she knows it's the truth. I was hyper with joy in the delivery room.

"My body's not the same."

"Neither's mine," I say, looking down. "Big fucking deal."

She runs her hands up my chest and around to the back of my neck, doing that thing where she scratches right at the base of my skull. It makes me hum; she knows this. "Yeah, but you're still hot," she says. "Look at you."

This is a promising comment. And okay, I try and look good for her. I run and do push-ups. I watch the beers. It's not like I'm on a diet or something, which come to think of it...

"You're gorgeous, you know. Now, even more so." I know she's been watching what she eats. Her body's changed since giving birth, yes. She's fuller in hip and breast and more rounded in belly and ass, but not less attractive—luscious, rather, and I just want my hands on her, want to feel her skin. I know guys who like them so skinny they look like they'll break, and then there are chubby chasers. God bless, to each his own, and all that. I like soft, a little curve. Or maybe I just like my girl. I don't even know the difference anymore.

She's got a couple buttons undone on the granny gown, and I reach down to undo a few more. She kisses me then—a real kiss with her tongue in my mouth and her hands in my hair, the first one in months. And as quickly as it starts, it ends.

"I'm just supposed to believe you were sitting downstairs masturbating?" she asks as she pulls away.

It's like I can see her mind click into gear. I'd gotten to the fourth button only to see a glimpse of that godforsaken nursing bra. When this is over, I am burning that thing.

"To thoughts of you, yeah," I say.

And then I hear one of the twins cry through the monitor on the bedside table.

She turns immediately, instinctively.

"I'll go," I say, grabbing her wrist. "Let me."

"No, it should be me," she says.

"If they're going to sleep through the night, shouldn't it be me? They smell you or something," I say, waving in the general direction of my enemy, the nursing bra.

"Okay," she says. She knows I'm right. And yes, I'm a man who'll do anything to get his kids to sleep through the night so he can have some of his wife's attention.

I try to get in there quickly, but I'm not fast enough and both of them are awake. Not to brag or anything, but I can change my twins in about a minute and a half flat.

But there's rocking and cuddling, and next thing I know I've fallen asleep in the rocking chair holding them, and so have they.

By the time I get them settled, it's nearly sunrise. I leave for work before anyone's up, fully intending to put in my time and make it home early tonight.

Have you ever had a dick boss? Of course you have. We all have. It just so happens to be my turn on the karmic wheel for that particular torture. He calls a team meeting starting at 6:30 p.m. Who the hell does that voluntarily? I was promoted into this position, and I'll be damned if I'm looking for a new job. Thankfully he doesn't play nice with others, and with a rep like that I give him a year, tops.

I call Elise to tell her I'll be late, and I can hear the doubt in her voice, the exhaustion too. The twins are crying in the background, so we hang up quickly. I sit through the endless meeting trying not to go crazy. Andrea, sitting across from me, catches my eye and mouths "Chill out," and I realize I'm bouncing my leg.

I have to get some stuff out before I go and even working quickly and accurately, it's late when I'm rolling home.

The moon is full and low on the horizon, a harvest moon, my dad used to call it. I've always thought they were cool, special, romantic, I guess. He told me crazy shit could happen during a moon like that.

All the lights are out when I turn down my drive. I knew they would be. And I know what I have to do.

I tiptoe through the dark house.

When I get to our bedroom door I pause, telling myself that tonight, I will not fail.

I kick off my shoes and socks, unbutton my shirt, and slip into the sheets in my undershirt and trousers. She's so warm in that flimsy granny gown again.

I kiss the back of her neck; she doesn't stir.

I nibble an earlobe and her hand swats me away like a fly.

"Els," I whisper in her ear.

She rolls to me and buries her face in my chest, clinging to sleep, her hand gripping my T-shirt.

I'm about to give in, give up. She's tired.

I kiss her forehead. "Wake up." I try a last time.

Her eyes flutter open. "There you are," I say.

I kiss her, but she's sleepy, languid—there's no *there*, there. I'm worried she's going to fall back to sleep on me. I don't think my ego, or hers, can take that right now.

I'm out of the bed then, reaching down and pulling her out too. She's cold, so I haul the bedspread off the bed and wrap it around her. She starts murmuring about being tired, but I give her the look. Don't pretend you don't know the look. It's best used sparingly, keeps the effectiveness fresh.

I lead her downstairs, making sure she doesn't trip in all her bundling. I'm thinking the walk will wake her. And I'm forming a plan. That's another thing if you want to be a husband. A plan will take you a long way. When I walk over to the French doors, she stalls.

"It's actually warmer outside than in the house. Come see," I say. It's one of those oddly warm fall nights, last breath of summer.

She's still wiping sleep out of her eyes.

"Look," I say, pointing at the full moon.

She's shrugged the bedspread off her shoulders, coming out of her cocoon, because it is pretty warm. Then she lets the blanket go in a puddle at her feet.

Her nightgown is nearly translucent in the moonlight. I can see every line of her body—the bright white and pale blue, like she's glowing. And I feel a little nuts with wanting her, kind of frenzied.

I grab her into my arms, kiss her, sloppy and needy. When I let her go after a minute, her shoulders are up to her ears. Jumping all over her is clearly not going to get me laid tonight.

I take a step back as I take the rest of the blanket from around her feet and lay it out on the ground.

The thing I have going for me here is that she's been harboring a little fantasy about this, about sex outside. She told me once. I think she was picturing a picnic on a summer day and lots of girly Jane Austen shit. This might do though—the moon, the night, me.

I've never been gladder that she wanted to live in the country, even with the commute. No neighbors can see us.

I tug my T-shirt over my head, down my arms and off in one quick motion. She steps away, finally fully waking, I think. I step forward, dropping my shirt, intent to have her in my arms again, but telling myself to take it slow.

"You want me to come after you?" I ask. Silly woman, if she thinks I don't want her, I am more than willing to show her she's wrong.

She's backing away from me, eyes on my face, my lips.

"I feel a little strange tonight," she says. "A little unhinged."

I can definitely work with unhinged.

"You want me to chase you?" I ask, moving slowly toward her. I am only half joking. "You want to be wanted?"

She laughs at me then, and I catch her up in my arms. It's only a minute before I have the nightgown up and over her head. She quickly discards my enemy the nursing bra, and she's standing there in panties that I'm already tugging off. When she's bare, she's like some otherworldly goddess from an old painting or something, standing before me, unreal and elementally beautiful, and I just want to feel her tits pressed up against my chest.

She reaches down to my belt, and feeling her unbuckle me,

unbutton me, unzip me—I almost lose it. She hasn't done that
in so long.

When she drops to her knees, I actually stop her. I know. But
I won't last long with her mouth on me. And it's just going to
make me rush everything until I'm inside her. But she's insistent
and when she leans forward and places a wet kiss right on the
tip, my resistance melts.

Then it's one long lick up the shaft, and she takes me in her
mouth. Then it's wet and heat and suction and I put my hands
in her hair, just feeling her move on me. Something's changed
though. Where did she pick this up? Is this like some womanly
wisdom passed from one new mother to another in all those
classes and books? Whatever it is, her mouth feels incredible,
and I stop her, and kneel down, lest this whole thing end much
earlier than either of us would like.

Don't judge my stamina. I've been deprived of my wife for
months now.

I kiss her then, rougher than I've probably ever kissed her.
And since turnabout is fair play, I lean her back and kiss right
under her navel. She's squirming to get away from me but it only
makes her body look divine, curvy flesh in icy pale, and I think
I might lose my mind. I kiss her right next to her hip, but there's
no denying she doesn't want me kissing her any lower.

I'm not going to push her now. Though I'd love nothing more
than to taste her; she smells incredible.

When I lift my head up, she pushes at my shoulder, and I roll
onto my back for her. She pushes me down into the blanket and
straddles my hips, her hot hands locked on my chest, and I think
I understand. It's her turn now.

With an immediate and wet slip of her hips, I'm sheathed to
the base. No preamble, no nothing, and it's overwhelming.

She is heat and home, both familiar and new, that feeling of
being engulfed. She is magnificent in the moonlight. I grab her

hips and push up into her with a groan, wanting more, always, but she goes still.

"Does that feel good?" she asks.

"Oh god. So fucking good."

"Then..." she says, and it's a statement. She takes first one of my hands off her waist and then the other and places them over my head. I lick her nipple—it is, after all, right in my face—and she gives me the look. Then she grinds down on me, and there's no way I'm moving my hands from over my head.

She rides me in the moonlight. And she looks amazing, feels fucking superb. But if I move, make even the slightest thrust, she stops. So I lie there in exquisite surrender, her motionless prey. And, I've gotta admit, I feel pretty wanted.

Her breasts bouncing above me, her hips grinding, the slick feel of her is heaven after missing her like I have. I smell grass and sex, and clench my hands in fists over my head to keep from touching her. She's looking down at where we're joined, watching as she moves me in and out with long hard strokes, and it almost kills me.

"You're watching us," I whisper. "Oh god, Els..." And I understand now. It's changed. Something we've done countless times is made new and better because of who we are to each other now. Because with the creation of our family, we will be bound together—always. And yet, here we are, still the same two lovers as when we first met.

And tonight she's in control.

She rides me until I can tell she's found it. She gasps, and then comes the hard grind as she falls onto my chest, skin on skin, mouth open on mine and I know she's close. I can move now, can bring my arms down to embrace her, to work her, to make her come. Until I too am falling into the night under the full moon with the only goddess I've ever worshipped, in my arms, above me.

PROOF

Mia Hopkins

Emma headed straight for the espresso machine behind the counter. She pulled herself two shots, slammed back the bitter liquid and felt herself slowly coming back to life.

"Hello, sleeping beauty," said Lexi, peeking her head through the office door. "Your team is already in the kitchen. Come on."

Emma let out a mighty yawn and followed her business partner into the office. Five years before, Emma and Lexi had opened the wildly successful Poppy Bakery in downtown Los Angeles. Blood, sweat and tears had gone into every detail. This week, they were facing their biggest project yet: catering the bread and desserts for the Governor's Ball following the Academy Awards. While Lexi would manage the day-to-day operations for the bakery, Emma would oversee the cakes, pastries and bread for the nearly two thousand guests.

"So, what kind of pirate crew do you have for me?" asked Emma as she tied on her apron.

"I got you Akira," said Lexi.

Trained in Paris and Tokyo, Akira was one of the most meticulous pastry chefs Emma had ever met. "Excellent," she said.

"And since you're making bread, I've invited an old favorite." Lexi put on her reading glasses and tied back her curly silver hair. "Lavoie."

Emma froze. "What?"

"Lucas Lavoie."

The name alone made Emma's skin tingle. "Oh," she said quietly.

Lexi looked sideways at Emma. "What's the matter?" she asked.

"Nothing's the matter," Emma said. She smoothed back her messy hair as best she could. "Nothing at all," she added. She smiled brightly at Lexi, even though her stomach had started to take a slow turn.

They walked from the office into the kitchen where Akira and Lucas were standing next to the bread station.

Had she known she was going to see Lucas today, Emma would have spent the night drinking wine and telling herself that she wasn't the same person she was when she was twenty-two. She would have reminded herself that she was now capable, confident and completely immune to men with an overabundance of French-Canadian handsomeness. She would have practiced her facial expressions in the bathroom mirror.

Lucas! How nice to see you again. Casual surprise.

Hi, Lucas! Thanks for coming to help us out. Friendly professionalism.

Hey, what's up? Neutral nonchalance.

But she hadn't had time to prepare. And now Lucas was here, standing in the middle of the kitchen, talking quietly to Akira about the difference between a starter and a leaven.

Emma felt the deep reverberation of his voice before she saw his face. She pursed her lips. How often had she daydreamed about seeing him again?

Lucas turned to face Lexi and Emma. High cheekbones, dark hair, short beard: he was the epitome of a gorgeous lumberjack. "My favorite California girls!" he exclaimed in his sexy accent. His smile was dazzling.

Before she knew what was happening, Emma had been scooped up along with Lexi into a big bear hug. Lucas was tall and crushed them against his broad chest, but what really struck Emma were his arms—sinuous, heavy with muscle and covered with a new brocade of tattoos. His skin was hot where it touched her wrist. The heat spread through her body like wildfire. When he put them down, Emma was trembling in her clogs as he gave both her and Lexi *un bec*, the *Québécois* kiss-kiss on each cheek.

Lexi turned to Akira and said, "Akira, this is Lucas Lavoie, owner-operator of Lavoie *Boulangerie* in Montreal. He is one of our dearest friends. Lucas helped Emma and me when we first opened."

As Lexi reviewed the menu with Akira, Emma glanced up at Lucas. He was grinning and staring right at her. The intensity of his blue-gray gaze forced her to look away. As she kept her eyes glued on the stainless-steel surface of the worktable, she felt out of control, aroused and embarrassed—everything that Lucas had made her feel the night before he got on a plane five years ago and left her behind without a text, a note or even *un bec* goodbye.

"So, Emma," he said quietly. "Ready to begin again?"

As she and Akira prepped the kumquat *coulis* sauce for the cheesecakes, Emma watched Lucas at the baker's bench. He threw a thin coating of flour across the steel table and drew out his ratios right on the surface. Then he went to the storage room for flour, salt, sugar and yeast. Simple ingredients, but in the hands of a bread baker—Lucas's hands—pure magic.

She tried not to stare as he worked. With efficiency and spare grace, he emptied a sack of flour into the mixer. The muscles in his arms swelled and slid beneath his skin. She had a flashback of what he looked like without his clothes on—his abs flexed, his chest covered in a thin sheen of sweat.

Akira turned to look at what she was staring at. "So what are you making?" he asked Lucas.

"*Ficelles* and *grissini* with bacon and parmesan. But small. Everything small."

"Bread for a dollhouse," said Akira.

"Exactly. It's going to be a pain in the ass."

They chuckled and Emma felt like the odd man out, overcome with awkwardness and an exasperated longing for Lucas that she couldn't shake.

"I'm going to start on the cheesecakes," she said to Akira. "Did you see the Valrhona chocolate in the storage room? Is it there?"

"The white chocolate? Yes. It's there."

In the cramped storage room, Emma loosened the top button of her chef's jacket and slid her hand underneath, pressing her palm against her pounding heart. Her nonsense with Lucas was nearly five years ago. She needed to get a grip. As she bent down among the cartons and boxes to search for the white chocolate, she heard the door open.

"Akira, did you say it was in the storage room or the utility room?" she said, scanning the bottom shelves.

"It's here."

Lucas's deep voice was soft, dampened in the enclosed space. He knelt down beside her on the tile and put his hand on her cheek. She could smell the flour on it, the clean, comforting scent of work and bread and home.

She started to move away. "You can't—"

With a kiss, Lucas made her swallow her words. His lips

were full and firm. The nerve endings in her lips fired bright sparkles into her brain. Overcome with surprise and pleasure, she parted her lips slightly, and he did the same. She felt the smooth, wet inner part of his mouth against hers. His short beard was soft against her chin.

Lost, Emma closed her eyes and felt the warmth of his fingers against her neck and throat. She curved into him, her body following the contour of his. His big hand slid underneath her chef's jacket and she felt it on her chest, pressing down against the fluttering of her heart. With a deep groan, he pulled her in closer.

He teased the inside curve of her lips. With the tip of his tongue, he flicked the point of her top lip like he might flick her clit if he were going down on her. Her pussy—not her brain—remembered what that felt like, and all of a sudden she was in his lap on the floor of the storage room. Still kissing him, she straddled him as he leaned back against the metal shelves, gripping her asscheeks and pressing her down on the enormous erection in his jeans.

This is insane, she thought. But she couldn't stop.

She dipped her tongue down into the sweet, musky darkness of his mouth like she were dipping a strawberry in chocolate, again and again until nothing but dark sweetness covered the berry, sealing in the juice.

With a groan, he broke their kiss. "I missed you so much, Emma," he whispered. "If only you knew how much I thought about this. About you."

She closed her eyes and let the sensations take her. Her hands clutching his rock-hard shoulders, she moved her hips up and down against the hard ridge of his cock.

"Did you find the white chocolate?" called Akira from the kitchen.

Emma's eyes flew open and she froze, the spell broken. She

cleared her throat. "Yes, I found it," she said loudly. "Thank you."

Slowly she stood up and steadied herself, buttoning up her jacket.

Lucas got to his feet and ran a hand through his hair.

"Thank god for aprons, huh?" he murmured, adjusting himself. For all his bearded manliness, he was blushing.

"I don't know why that happened," she said, avoiding his eyes.

"I do," Lucas whispered, following her out. "And if I survive this shift with you, I want to make it happen again."

Twelve hours later, the refrigerators were full of tiny cheese-cakes. The proofing boxes were full of tiny loaves of bread made from a wild yeast starter that Lucas had brought with him from Canada. Fatigue blurring her vision, Emma locked the front and back doors of the bakery and waved goodbye to Akira as he rode away on his bike. Lexi and the rest of the crew were long gone.

"Back at the *boulangerie*, I've been experimenting with longer proofing times," Lucas said as he walked Emma back to her loft a few blocks away. The sun was setting. After a steamy kitchen, the cool open air was a welcome change.

"Twelve hours is a long time to proof," said Emma.

"Some dough just needs more time to rise," he said with a smirk. "We'll have a big bake-off tomorrow morning. You'll see. The flavor will be remarkable."

Traffic lurched down Spring Street. Loft dwellers, dog walkers, homeless people and patrol cops crowded the sidewalk. Emma and Lucas walked past a sidewalk cafe and a few women sitting at the tables nearly got whiplash checking out Lucas, which made Emma feel both disgusted and perversely smug. A late winter wind kicked up between the buildings. Emma put her hands in the pockets of her hoodie.

"You're cold?" asked Lucas. "This is nothing."

"I'm from Southern California. This is cold to me."

Lucas put his arm around her shoulders and held her close. "I'll keep you warm, *ma mie*."

"*Ma mie*. What does that mean?" she asked. His body heat seeped through his clothes.

"It's very old-fashioned. It means 'my darling.' Also, it means bread. The soft part. Inside the crust."

They arrived at her building, an old bank that had been converted into lofts.

"Let me come up with you," Lucas said.

Emma closed her eyes, trying to pretend that the sound of his voice didn't send all the blood in her veins rushing straight to her clit. "I don't know if that would be a good idea."

"It's a fantastic idea. I assure you."

"I had a crush on you a long time ago. That's it," she said softly. Lucas was the best sex she'd ever had, bar none. No one else had ever come close.

He put his arms around her and whispered in her ear, "That's not it and you know it. Please, Emma. Let me come upstairs."

Lips locked in a ravenous kiss, they stumbled into her bedroom. Lucas untied Emma's ponytail and ran his fingers through her dark hair. He stroked her face, his fingers skimming the burning surface of her skin. Under the spell of his touch, her face became a new erogenous zone. Her nerves pulsed with pure pleasure.

He undressed her in a heartbeat. After she unbuttoned his chef's jacket and pulled his T-shirt over his head, she looked up at him. He was a fantasy come true, all hard muscle and taut skin. A healthy amount of dark chest hair couldn't hide his well-defined pecs or the ridges of his abs. His arms were glorious. A full-sleeve tattoo swirled from his wrist to the cap of muscle on his shoulder like the arm guard on a gladiator.

She stared. "What is your tattoo?"

"Lots of things." As he smiled at her, a lock of dark hair fell over his forehead. He pointed to designs embedded in the tattoo. "These are flowers from the flag of Montreal, a rose and a thistle. Dragon scales here, because I was born in the year of the dragon. And this. Do you recognize this?"

He pointed to a splash of burnt orange on the inside of his forearm.

"No. What is it?" she asked quietly, tracing the design with her fingertip.

"A reminder of your bakery," he said. "Where I was happy. A California poppy."

He pushed her gently onto the bed and kissed her until she was breathless. He kneaded her breasts with his big hands and then proceeded to lick and suck on her nipples until her mind went blank, overloaded with sensation.

When he kissed her again, her legs fell open and his hand slid down the center of her body before it stopped at her sex. After he pressed the heel of his palm gently against her soft hair, he curled his fingertips against the achingly hot, slick flesh between her legs. She grabbed his shoulders and shuddered into his kiss.

"You're so sexy, Emma," he whispered. "I'm going to devour you."

As a baker, Lucas did everything by feel. He knew when dough was ready by the way it stretched and pulled between his fingers. His hands were strong and self-assured. Touch was his sharpest sense.

In silence, Emma looked down and watched his fingertips glide over her tender flesh. He placed his thumb and forefinger on either side of her pussy lips and opened her up slowly, revealing hot pink folds that deepened in color toward her center.

Still holding her open, he lowered his lips to her and she felt his warm breath wash over her aching clit. Moisture gathered at the entrance of her pussy and he lapped it up.

"Oh god," she whispered. She buried her hands in his thick hair and arched her back into the mattress.

His tongue carved through her as he licked up and down the inner lips of her pussy. She could feel his beard brushing against her. He was slow and exacting, each lash of his tongue pulling intense pleasure from her body. Emma could hear her breathing quicken and become raspy.

He besieged her. When the tip of his tongue finally circled her swollen clit, Emma's long, strangled moan bounced off the bare concrete walls of her loft. At the same time, Lucas sank a thick finger into her pussy, keeping it straight as he pressed deeper and deeper into her heat.

"So tight," he said. "Yes. Grip me. Like that."

She did, pulling at him as hard as she could as he began to ravish her clit with his tongue. With his other hand, he reached up and gripped her breast, kneading it hard, rolling her nipple between his thumb and forefinger until rapture slid against the sweet edge of pain.

Still working her with his hot tongue, he pushed a second finger into her, stretching her, pulling back and forth until the friction began to set off deep tremors inside her. The minutes ticked by and Lucas's constant rhythm summoned layers upon layers of pleasure. Emma dug her hands into the bedsheets and shut her eyes tight, panting, trying to hold back the enormous orgasm that he was building inside her.

"Emma," he said, breathless. He pulled back. "I feel like I'm going to die."

Trembling, she sat up and helped him take off his jeans and boxers. His cock sprang up at her, thick and dusky and glistening, the head swollen and purple. She threw him playfully back against the bed. As his legs dangled off the edge of the mattress, she straddled his chest and took him into her mouth, enjoying the feeling of his big cock sliding against her lips.

He grabbed her hips and moved his head between her legs. She slid off his cock and squealed, trying to wiggle away, but he was so much bigger and stronger than her that she had no choice except to endure it when he lifted his hot mouth to her pussy.

"Sixty-nine is so weird," she said, still struggling. "My ass is right there. In your face."

"Are you crazy? This is fucking sexy," he growled. "Suck me. God, I'm begging you."

She did. She sucked hard on the head of his cock and kneaded the rigid base of his shaft with both hands. He tasted clean, of salt and pure sex, and she couldn't get enough. His flavor and scent existed in the deepest part of her memory, and as she went down on him, memories of their one wild night came flooding back to her along with years of pent-up longing and regret. At the same time, he feasted on her. The wet, clicking sound of his tongue on her clit drove her insane. His superior sense of touch seemed to tell him when to back off and when to push harder. The dark shadow of her orgasm grew more powerful, but still Lucas wouldn't let her come.

When she began to tongue his balls, he hissed at last and pulled away, gasping for breath. He looked at her with a raised eyebrow and Emma pointed to her nightstand. Lucas took out a condom and rolled it on as she watched. The latex strained around his thick shaft.

He picked her up and placed her head carefully on her pillow. Their eyes still locked together, she spread her legs wide open for him. He took his cock in his hand and slid his glans up and down her delicate flesh, smearing her arousal over them both.

"You are the best lover I've ever had, Emma," he whispered. He leaned forward and the pink lips of her pussy crowned the head of his cock.

"I never thought I'd see you again," she replied, pressing her hands against his rigid pecs. Her fingers looked slim and delicate against his chest. She lifted her hips upward to meet him, and he moaned, his chest rising and falling as he struggled to keep his composure.

"I'm here now," he said. "I'm not going anywhere."

He raised himself up on his arms, showing off the beautiful sinews in his shoulders and biceps. He flexed his ass and slid into her inch by inch, raising himself up and back each time so that she could feel her pussy stretching around him. He gave her more and more with each thrust until she thought she was going to die of ecstasy, here on the end of Lucas Lavoie's glorious cock. She had to admit it wouldn't be a bad way to go.

When he was halfway in, he reached down and drew circles on her tender, aching clit. Slick with moisture, the pad of his thumb slid over the tiny button and she began to shiver around him.

"You're so beautiful," he whispered.

He kissed her once more, closed his eyes and slammed home. He pulled out nearly all the way and rammed into her again, crushing her body beneath his.

"Yes," she said again, gripping his asscheeks. "Like that."

Lucas began to fuck her hard. Her pussy, stretched to its limit around his shaft, was stuffed so tightly that she couldn't move as he thrust into her, again and again, smacking his balls against her. His hair grew damp with sweat. Lips parted, he panted and grunted above her, fighting for breath. Outside, a winter wind rattled the windows. Inside, she and Lucas were hot and sweaty, fucking like animals, pushing the bed sideways across the floor.

With muscles built up from years of hauling flour and kneading dough, Lucas picked her up off the bed and, still buried inside her, carried her to the concrete wall by her bed. She wrapped her arms around his shoulders. Pinned against a cold wall and Lucas's searing hot body, she began to lose herself: where she was, what she was doing, even her name until Lucas leaned down and whispered it in her ear along with sexy filth in two languages.

"Emma. I love your sweet little pussy, *ma chère*."

She couldn't remember the night she'd spent with Lucas five years ago. The old impressions that flashed through her mind—the taste of him, the feeling of coming hard against his tongue, the shame of losing control—became erased the moment he began to pound into her, pushing the air in and out of her lungs as he pinned her against the wall.

Then he pressed his thumb against her clit, and she was lost.

She came at once. Her screams bounced against the high ceilings of the loft and she convulsed violently around him, again and again, milking him with long, agonizing spasms.

When her climax finally subsided, Lucas, wild-eyed, pulled out of her carefully and turned her around. Panting and dripping, she placed her hands flat against the concrete. He pushed down on the center of her back and bent her forward until her ass was in the air.

He kneaded her asscheeks and pulled them apart just far enough to make her squirm. She was almost a foot shorter than him, so he had to bend his knees as he fed his cock back into her. The smell of sweat and sex and latex filled the room and Emma drank it in the way she drank him in, all of her senses hungry for more.

"Touch yourself," he commanded.

She slid a hand down between her legs and rubbed her clit as Lucas slid deeper. He gathered her hair in his fist and pulled her head back. The pain coaxed fresh spurts of arousal from her pussy and Emma felt the improbable stirrings of a second orgasm at the base of her spine.

Holding on to her hip, he began to ride her hard, smacking

into her ass with the rigid muscles of his abs. He changed his angle and the head of his cock dug against the front wall of her pussy, hitting her G-spot with laser precision.

"There," he whispered. He quickly found his rhythm. Holding her in a lock that she couldn't—and didn't want to—escape from, Lucas pounded her until she began to feel herself losing control again.

He pulled her hair again, harder this time, putting a deep bend in her spine like the curve of a bow.

"Now, Emma. Come now," he growled.

Her pussy exploded again, crushing him in another series of merciless convulsions. Lucas climaxed in silence, his hand grasping her hip, his cock thickening and pulsing inside her. Blood rushed in her ears as they took the long, sweet ride together.

Afterward, he collapsed against her, his solid chest pressed against her back, his arms wrapped around her waist.

"God," he gasped. "Oh god."

They stood together for a full minute as they caught their breath. Slowly, he slid out of her and turned her around in his arms.

She looked up at him as he held her. "I missed you," she whispered.

He brushed away the tears on her cheeks. "I missed you, too," he said.

At four in the morning, Emma's alarm clock went off. She reached up and hit the snooze button. As she rolled back over, Lucas took her again in his arms, pinning her to the mattress and pressing his insistent early morning hard-on against her belly.

"Good morning, *ma mie*," he whispered, gently biting her earlobe.

He reached down and brushed his fingertips against her hypersensitive clit. At the command of his touch, her body began to well up again. In less than a minute, she was slick and hot and ready.

"I want you," Lucas said. "Then and now."

His words brought her mind into sharp focus. She reached down and took his wrist, pulling his hand away from her.

He opened his eyes. "What's wrong?"

Her heart squeezed in her chest. "I always regretted sleeping with you. I thought you didn't want me."

"What?" Lucas said. "No, my god. That is not it at all." He sat up.

"Then what?"

He brushed his dark hair away from his eyes. "I was so in love with you. But I had nothing, Emma. A temporary visa that was about to expire. No money in my pocket. What could I offer you?"

She looked down at his hand in hers. "Yourself. A text. A note. Something."

"I thought you would be better off without me. But I was wrong to treat you that way." He brought her hand to his lips. "It's been five years and I can't get you out of my mind. I told myself when I got on the plane, if you weren't seeing anyone, I would try to make things right between us. Emma, I want you. Let me prove it to you."

"How can this possibly end well? You live in Montreal. I live in Los Angeles."

He gave a little Gallic shrug. "There's an old saying. *'L'absence est à l'amour ce qu'est au feu le vent; il éteint le petit, il allume le grand.'* It means that absence in love is like wind on fire. It blows out small fires, but it makes big fires grow bigger."

She sighed. "That's stupid. Just because you make it sound pretty by saying it in French doesn't make it less stupid."

He took her hand and wrapped it around the shaft of his cock. "Well," he said with a wink, "I myself am stupid in both English and French. At least you can't accuse me of misrepresentation."

Two hours later, flushed and smiling, they staggered into the bakery and fired up the ovens. The elemental smell of fresh bread filled Emma's nose as she began to assemble the white-chocolate petals for the cheesecakes. When the first tiny loaf came out of the oven, Lucas tore it open and fed it to her. Its crackling crust gave way to a hot, elastic center. They shared bites of bread, cups of espresso and more kisses until the morning crew came in.

At noon, the catering truck came to pick up the bread and desserts for the Governor's Ball. Akira, Emma and Lucas celebrated with sparkling wine and ham and butter sandwiches made with Lucas's amazing bread.

That afternoon, Emma drove Lucas across town to Santa Monica where he was staying. On Ocean Drive, the fresh sea air kissed her face as Lucas ran his hand through her hair. The bittersweet happiness of being close to him again filled her veins like a drug.

"I'm in love with you," he said.

"You can't be serious. You're just visiting."

"Who said I was just visiting?" he said. He pointed to a busy street corner. "This is me. Stop here."

She pulled up to the curb in front of an empty storefront whose windows were covered with brown paper.

"You want proof that I'm serious about us?" Lucas asked. "Look up, *ma mie*."

"What?"

Emma looked through the windshield. Above the store window hung a sign, done up in blue and white. Emma gasped as she read it.

Lucas smiled. "They told me Americans can't pronounce *boulangerie*. So I settled on 'Lavoie Bakery.' I don't think it has the same ring, but what do I know? Whatever the case, we open in July."

She was confused. "So...you're opening...another branch?"

"No, *ma mie*. I sold the one in Montreal. This is home now." He took her hand and kissed it. "It's been a long time for us, Emma. Tell me. Will you be my girlfriend?"

She was quiet for a moment, too overcome with emotion to respond.

"What do you think?" he asked. The vulnerability in his eyes made her heart ache.

This is insane, she thought.

"Yes," she said.

Their kiss outlasted the sunset over the Pacific Ocean. By the time they made it out of the car and upstairs into his apartment, the sky was deep blue and aching for stars.

"You know," she said, unbuckling his belt as he walked backward into the bedroom. "'Lavoie' is no walk in the park for Americans to pronounce either."

"Too bad," he said with a smile. "The sign's already paid for. Everyone will just have to learn."

THE ONE WHO CAME INSTEAD

Tamsin Flowers

She came from New York, but it seemed to Karen that Paris was the coldest city on the planet. At least whenever she'd been here, which was only twice. She pulled her coat collar up around her neck against a wind that continued to insinuate itself through all the layers of her clothing. On a dull day, the city turned a uniform shade of gray, though it was never for a moment anything less than breathtaking.

Would it be the same if I lived here, she wondered, *or would a winter's day simply make me long for spring, with its sunshine and blossoms?*

The Centre Pompidou loomed up ahead of her like a giant birdcage emerging from the mist. It was larger than she remembered but essentially the same—a giant grid of steel girders and pipes with a glass tube of escalators snaking up the side. She remembered riding up those escalators seven years ago, leaning back against Elliot's chest as he stood on the step behind her. The view should have been stunning by the time they reached the sixth floor, only it had been foggy that day as well. But they weren't there for the view—they were there for the art. And for each other—on one of the broad galleries, looking out toward the mist-shrouded spires of Notre Dame, Elliot had kissed her for the first time.

She could still feel the pressure of his lips against hers, taste the salt on them from the croque monsieur he'd had for lunch. Seven years had passed and she could still remember what they'd eaten for lunch that day. She couldn't, however, recall whose idea it had been to come back here, seven years on, when they would both be thirty.

"Whatever happens, Karen," Elliot had said. "Whether we're still together or single or with other people, we should still come back here. Just to remember this day. Just to see how the other's doing."

"But we'll know that, if we're still together," she'd said, convinced, as one always is at the beginning, that the thing's going to last forever.

It hadn't lasted forever. Two years was all they'd managed before his job and her family had torn them apart. It had ended grumpily and for two years after that Karen had believed she never wanted to lay eyes on him again. But time thaws even the coldest cut and now she wondered if he would remember their promise that day. She didn't expect him to be here—even if he did remember, he wasn't going to fly thousands of miles on a first-love whim. She was only here because her job involved European travel and it had been easy to jiggle her schedule to accommodate this particular date. To be in Paris on the day she was supposed to be.

So did that mean she secretly hoped he would come?

Her heart was pounding by the time she reached the top of the fifth escalator. Every man ahead of her or behind her on the way up received a second glance. Just in case he was Elliot. She wondered how much he would have changed in seven years.

Would he be easy to spot, instantly recognizable? She looked the same. She hadn't changed her hair and if there were some tiny crow's feet appearing at the corners of her eyes, they weren't visible from a distance.

She walked out into the wide gallery, almost scared to run her eyes along the length of the windows until they rested at the very spot where she and Elliot had exchanged that first kiss. There was no one there. A harassed-looking woman with two young children battled her buggy onto the down escalator. An elderly couple were whispering together over coffee at one of the tables. She didn't remember there being a café here before, but it made sense to make the most of the view.

Karen checked her watch. She was ten minutes early, so why not have a coffee and stare out for a while into the gray mists? All the while, she kept checking the top of the escalator and the line at the counter. Just in case Elliot appeared after all. The coffee scalded her tongue, but she was too nervous to take her time with it. She finished the drink quickly and then paced slowly up and down along the window for a few more agonizing minutes. When she next looked at her wrist, it was a quarter after the hour. He wasn't coming and she'd never really believed that he would.

But still she scanned the faces of the men coming up the escalators toward her as she snaked down. Between the fourth floor and third floor, a man passed her who made her look again. It wasn't Elliot but there was something in his face she knew.

"Karen?"

She had already turned to look back up when he spoke to her. A tall man with an abundance of dark hair was running down the up escalator toward her, so she started walking up toward him. When they were level with each other, she knew that she knew him.

"Go down," he said. "I'll meet you on floor three."

She stopped walking up and let the escalator carry her down, while he ran the rest of the way up his side and then back down the other to catch her.

"You probably don't remember me," he said, somewhat out of breath as he came up to her in the empty gallery on the third floor.

"I don't remember your name but I knew you, didn't I, when I was seeing Elliot?"

He nodded.

"I'm Tom."

He stuck out a hand to shake at the same moment that Karen stepped forward to greet him with a kiss. A second's awkwardness ensued and they both laughed.

"It's weird that you're here," said Karen.

"You were expecting Elliot."

"You know? Elliot told you?" For some reason Karen's heart was pounding again. Elliot hadn't forgotten. "Is he here? Is he coming?"

But a fleeting expression on Tom's face told her he wasn't.

"Let's sit down," said Tom.

"Have you seen Elliot?" said Karen, letting Tom lead her to a clear acrylic bench.

Tom shook his head.

"I haven't seen Elliot for ages. He told me about your promise as soon as you got back from Paris. But, no, he won't be coming. He's got four kids under three or three kids under four…"

Karen had to laugh. She couldn't see smooth, sleek Elliot as a dad.

"You're joking?"

Tom shook his head. "It's very painful for him."

"So you're here as his proxy?"

Tom's expression became serious.

"I'm here, one hundred percent, on my own account."

Karen stared at him. She'd always thought Tom was good looking and all of a sudden it hit her that he was far more handsome than Elliot had ever been.

"What exactly do you mean by that?" she said, slowly drawing out the words.

"When Elliot told me about this arrangement you'd made I was intrigued. For some reason the date stuck in my mind. I always wondered if you'd both come."

"And you thought you'd come along as third wheel?"

He picked up Karen's hand in one of his and she started slightly, caught unaware by the gesture.

"I always imagined coming to meet you here instead of him."

Karen took a moment to fully understand what he was saying.

"So does Elliot know you're here?"

"Listen, don't take this the wrong way, Karen, but I think Elliot forgot all about it within a couple of months. I mean, you broke up years ago."

Karen looked down at the strong, tanned hand that was still holding hers. Sculpted fingers that were warm to the touch. And dry. She couldn't bear a man with clammy hands. Then she looked up at Tom's face—chestnut eyes, nose a little large but a beautiful mouth with dark lips, a clean strong jawline. Her gaze snapped back to his eyes, which were locked on hers. Deep pools of caramel warmth.

She cleared her throat.

"Are you with someone?" She knew how the question sounded, what it might imply, but she had to ask it before she sank any deeper into those eyes.

"No." His voice sounded shaky compared with before.

"And you came here, just on the off chance I might have remembered?"

He dragged his eyes away from hers, just for a second.

"Hell, this is embarrassing," he said. "Yup, three and a half thousand miles just on the off chance."

His discomfort brought a smile of sympathy to her face, but he let go of her hand.

"God, you must think I'm a lunatic."

"I'm charmed."

"Really?"

"Really."

Over the course of this exchange her fingers had wound around his. She found she liked touching his hand. It felt comforting.

"What happens now?" he said.

"Are you staying nearby?" she asked.

PARIS IS FOR LOVERS. That was the T-shirt slogan that leapt out at Karen from a hundred souvenir shop windows. And as she and Tom walked arm-in-arm through the streets back to his hotel, anyone might be forgiven for assuming they already were.

They didn't say much to each other. There would be plenty of time to catch up later. But now was all about the chemistry. Tom pulled her hand into his coat pocket and in an instant the gray sky and damp mist that clung to her hair in droplets didn't matter. In that moment Paris had all the charm of a spring day, making Karen smile at herself in a shop window reflection.

Tom's hotel wasn't far away. He was staying in a small boutique hotel on the Rue de Rivoli. Karen didn't notice the hotel name as they went inside. She felt as if she'd drunk a large glass of wine, far too quickly, although the only thing she'd had all day was coffee. Giddy was the word for it. Giddy and excited— and just a tiny bit scared as they went up in the elevator. Not scared of Tom. Just scared of her own potential to fuck this up. Scared she'd misinterpreted what was happening here.

Tom opened the door to his room with a key card, ushering her inside with a shy smile.

"Let me take your coat," he said.

He hung it in the wardrobe and then went to the minibar.

"I think I need a drink," he said. "You?"

Karen nodded. "Please. A glass of wine."

They stood looking out of the window as they sipped wine from bathroom tumblers. Tom turned to face her and took the glass from her hand.

"Karen..." He put the two glasses down on a low table. "Is this...? Are you...?" He cleared his throat nervously. "If this is too fast for you..."

She knew what he was trying to say and she shook her head.

"It's not too fast, Tom. It's been seven years in the making."

With that she'd granted him permission, and he didn't waste any time. He wrapped his arms around her and pulled her in close against his chest, gazing down at her as if he was seeing her for the first time in seven years.

"You haven't changed a bit," he said, but she couldn't answer as his face bent lower and his lips brushed hers. Desire started to uncoil low in her belly. She was very conscious of the warmth of his hands on her back, the taste of wine on his breath. With a murmur, she kissed him back, entwining her hands at the back of his neck. His lips moved slowly against hers, tugging gently as he explored the shape of her mouth.

Karen's hips pressed forward against him and her back softened as she melted into the kiss. This was so absolutely not what she'd been expecting but now that it was happening, there seemed a certain inevitability about it. She pushed her tongue out for a taste of his and his mouth opened. His tongue snaked against hers and her insides tightened. The kiss intensified as he explored her insistently, claiming her lips, her teeth, her tongue as his prize. She wanted to drink him in. Each new breath tasted of him, intoxicating her far more than the scant mouthful of wine she'd drunk.

Tom groaned and staggered slightly as he broke off the kiss. Karen gasped.

"Oh god, Karen," he said. There was a break in his voice.

He dropped to his knees in front of her and as she steadied herself with one hand on the back of a chair, he placed his hands on her hips. He paused to look up at her and she nodded. She couldn't think of anything she wanted more than to feel Tom's long, strong fingers undoing the button at the top of her jeans. He drew the zipper down slowly. Karen wasn't sure her legs would hold her upright for much longer and, as if he'd read her mind, he maneuvered her back until she could sit down on the bed.

He unzipped her ankle boots with the same slow deliberation and tugged them off, rolling down each sock as soon as he'd put the boot aside. Karen leaned back on her elbows on the dark-red coverlet. Her breathing was ragged as he brought his hands back to the waistband of her jeans. His fingers were shaking. Karen closed her eyes as he peeled away the tight denim. Her panties came off at the same time and she raised her hips to make it easier for him. The shock of cool air on her skin sent a shiver up her spine. Then Tom's warm palms flat against the outer surfaces of her legs sent another shiver running through her, this time of a totally different kind.

His hands slid around to the inside of her thighs and he gently parted her legs.

"Damn it, you're beautiful," he said and she felt the whisper of his breath in the vortex between her legs. Of course, she was already wet. She had been before they'd even reached the hotel and their long lingering kiss had done nothing to stem the tide. He ran one finger along the cleft between her lips and then drew it back down with increased pressure to open them up. Then he pushed a finger high up into her. The shock of pleasure was like an electric current, making her yelp. He quickly withdrew and she felt instantly bereft.

"Are you okay...?"

"Don't stop—it was good."

She opened her eyes to see his reassured smile and then he kissed the softest skin in the crease at the top of her leg. But he didn't replace the finger he'd taken out. Instead, Karen felt the tip of his tongue pressing softly against the side of her lips. His fingers spread her open and his tongue followed them into the deepest recess. Her hips shifted to the edge of the bed and she let her legs flop even wider apart. As his tongue moved slowly in and out of her, his nose rubbed against the fleshy folds of her pussy. It felt unbelievably good and she was torn between wanting it to go on forever and needing to feel the weight of his cock between her legs.

His tongue slipped out of her and was quickly replaced by two long fingers. He fucked her with his hand while his tongue sought out buried treasure higher up.

"I used to dream of doing this," he said, his words almost muffled as his mouth closed around her clit.

His tongue found what it was looking for and traced a circular path around his prize. Karen stretched away, arching her back to thrust her pelvis forward. Suction made her gasp loudly as she clutched for handfuls of the covers. The tongue that had felt so gentle in her mouth felt rough against the sensitive skin of her clit, rasping across it possessively, pulling and pressing. His mouth matched the movement of her hips as his fingers worked inside her. She felt completely open to his touch, pushing up to meet him, letting him know with soft moans how much pleasure he was giving her.

His tongue moved back and his teeth nipped painfully, closing sharply around her clit. With his free hand, he pinned her hips to the bed to stop her moving. She was still while his jaws roved, rolling her engorged clit between his teeth, pressing down harder until she had to scream. She grabbed at handfuls of his hair, not to push his head away but to thrust it harder, deeper between her legs.

The orgasm that ripped through her was just the first. As she lay panting on the bed, recovering from a climax that had shaken her to her very core, Tom stood up and wiped his face on his shirtsleeve.

Karen blinked. The bulge in his trousers made her feel instantly ready.

"I want you," she said.

"I'm yours."

Slowly he unbuttoned his shirt and shrugged it back over his shoulders. His torso was slender, though still muscular, and his skin was pale. There was only a sprinkling of hair on his chest and his nipples stood out like pink smudges that instantly made Karen want to lick them. He pulled the end of his belt taut to undo it and the rattle of the belt buckle sent another shiver through Karen's still pulsing depths. His trousers dropped to the floor and he stood in front of her in white shorts, his cock straining out against the fabric.

"Let me," she said.

She slid forward on the bed until she was sitting on the edge.

"Come here."

He stepped closer and she reached out to touch his chest. He bent and kissed her on the mouth as gently as before, while she reached around to slip her hands into the back of his waistband. Undressed, he smelled so good. More than good. A delicious mingle of sweat and cologne and musk. Elemental male scent, with just a hint of her own smell added to the mix. Bringing her hands around the sides of his hips, she lowered his shorts, tugging at the waistband to free his cock and letting them drop to the floor. He stepped out of them, kicking the garment to one side.

Karen pulled her mouth away from his and put a hand against his chest to straighten him up. She took a long, hard look at his long, hard cock, bobbing in front of her face, and she liked what she saw very much. She reached out to touch it and it twitched as she wrapped her palm around it. She could feel the throb of a dark-blue vein that ran the length of its underside and she succumbed to a sudden compulsion to feel that same pulse with her tongue.

Tom put his hands on her shoulders as she sucked him into her mouth. The skin of the head of his cock was soft and a little salty. She searched out the tiny slit in the end and was rewarded with an even saltier taste of precome. Underneath, she found the ridge of the blue vein, bulging softly from the hard surface. She ran her tongue along its length, twisting her head so she could reach right down to the base, letting her tongue dart across the velvety skin and skitter all the way back up.

Tom grunted, rocking back on his heels. Karen sucked the length of his cock back into her mouth, stretching her neck out as she felt its blunt end hitting her palate. He whimpered and his hips jerked forward as he fucked her mouth. Karen slipped her arms around his waist to grab his buttocks, guiding him in and out, backward and forward, first quickly and then slowing it down so she could work him with her tongue. A trail of his salty juice trickled down Karen's chin and she brought a hand around to cup his balls, applying soft pressure as she kept him moving in her mouth. Gradually, she increased the intensity of her sucking—she was so turned on, she practically wanted to swallow him entirely. But she held herself back, building his pleasure, massaging him with her tongue, playing her teeth along his length. Above her, she sensed his back arching as he emitted a long, low moan. Her tongue moved faster as she pulled him deeper into her mouth but he pulled back against her.

"I need to be inside you," he said. "I don't want to come yet, not until I'm inside you."

Reluctantly, she let him withdraw.

"Take this off," he said, tugging at the hem of the T-shirt Karen was still wearing.

He helped her raise it over her head. She wasn't wearing a bra and before the garment was clear she felt his mouth on one of her breasts. His tongue circled her nipple and then sucked it hard, pulling on it until Karen gasped. He used a hand to do the same to her other breast until Karen was moaning with need.

He pushed her up the bed and then reached out to the bedside cabinet.

"I've got a condom," he said.

She nodded, thankful that one of them could still think rationally. She knew she would have let him fuck her without one. He ripped open the package and she helped him put it on. They both fumbled and it seemed to take forever but finally he was ready and he pushed her down onto her back on the bed. She opened her legs and guided him in as his mouth found hers.

It immediately felt right. Like a key entering a lock, the fit was perfect. He filled her and as he started to move slowly forward and back, waves of pleasure began rippling up through her like pulses of electric current. His tongue claimed hers and she raised her legs to wrap them around his waist. Ever so gradually, he built up speed, pushing himself deeper inside her with each thrust. She pushed back with her hips, opening herself up for him. The friction of his chest rubbing against her engorged nipples sent another flurry spiraling through her.

When he dropped his head to kiss the side of her neck, she reached a point of no return. The sharp dig of his teeth at the crook between neck and shoulder heralded a fierce cry as every shock wave of pleasure merged into an orgasm that tore through her, ripping her wide open, exposing all of her vulnerability and need. Her hips pushed up harder as his ground down on her, and he surged deeper still as her muscles closed tight around him. He made a noise that was part growl, part moan, back arched, still pushing against her as he came in response to the contractions inside her.

He slumped down on her, panting, their chests rising and falling in unison as they struggled for depleted oxygen. She lost herself in his deep-brown eyes and he smiled. Their hips were still flexing against each other as their climaxes receded. She felt his cock deflating inside her and as it slipped out she experienced another whisper of pleasure that made her giggle. He rolled off her and then pulled her across him so her head and one shoulder were on his chest. One of his arms wrapped protectively around her.

"Wow!"

It was all he needed to say and she nodded in agreement.

They lay like that for a while until he needed to move his arm.

"Do you still wish it had been Elliot?" he asked.

Elliot. The one who got away.

"Do you always ask silly questions?" she replied.

Now they could talk. Now they could catch up on the seven years gone by.

IN THE DARK, SO BRIGHT

Laila Blake

She was the first person I saw that night, standing across the room, and the shock of recognition fired through my system. I hadn't wanted to go, had pushed and bullied and jostled myself off my sofa and away from the joint I could have rolled. I never liked industry parties, full of people desperate to be seen. Performers do better in groups of normal people, I feel.

The music was bad, like anything that tries to appeal to the broadest possible spectrum, desperate not to exclude or offend anyone—lukewarm and stale, like the beer served at the bar. There were some other people I knew; nobody I wanted to talk to. But the flash of her profile haunted me, more than I was ready to face.

I found her again, once I had my drink, saw her standing in a group, laughing, gesticulating with those fingers I used to admire—long and strong for a woman, agile in their expression. Her hair was different, and she wore more expensive clothes, but she looked just the same as she did a few years ago. She still didn't use any makeup I could see, still wore flats on a party floor littered with clicking heels.

I remembered the wave of curiosity that had washed me to her shores when I first saw her. We were younger then; I was still in my twenties and I think she was just nineteen. She was stocky and tall, heavyset, with limbs and torso as big as mine, and maybe stronger. She moved her body with every word she spoke, hands and shoulders and face expressing her thoughts louder than any voice could. There was a strange grace to her, a curious attraction.

I'd wanted to fuck her even before I knew her name, wanted to feel those strong hands around my cock, wanted to find out what it would be like to eschew all standards I'd grown to accept, in which the first thing a girl had to be was smaller than. Smaller than me, smaller than her friend next to her.

I was drawn to this girl, this woman, who occupied space so confidently.

She was a songwriter, I found out by listening in. She ordered red wine, not a beer or a cocktail, and when her group dispersed I made my move. We talked until our feet were aching, until we found a table in the thinning venue. We talked all night, talked about music and poetry and about the stars. We talked about the intricate relationship between colors and sounds, about sex and obsessions. We compared tattoos and tried to express in words the way something so painful could feel so good. After her fourth glass of wine, she told me she liked to be fucked the way she wrote her songs: raw and hard and honest. No icing, no hollow words and no sugar-bow on top.

I remembered my cock was straining against my jeans. I wanted to pull her out into the night, wanted to fuck her up against the wall and on the taxi ride home. I drifted in and out of focus, then, the way you do when you want to do two things at once: listen and try to find a smooth way to interest her in spending the night.

And then she started talking about her boyfriend. We were

both drunk by then, and she was resting her chin on her hands, looking soft and strong in the most perplexing contradiction. He studied law, thought her passions were a waste of time, didn't like it when she wore bright colors.

I didn't know what to say, wanted to find him and punch him and take her home, as a victor's spoils. Instead I got angry like the dick I was. She had wasted my evening. All this time I spent talking to her, I could have found someone to fuck and now the party was over, only some sad losers left. Losers like me, maybe, who bet on the wrong game.

I left her there, didn't even ask how she would get home.

I never realized how strongly she stuck in my mind all the same. Maybe I never understood the real reason I got so angry, maybe even stupid younger me got on some level that in the hours of drinking and talking, I'd started writing songs in my head for this girl I had only just met.

And here she was again, more beautiful than before, settled into herself in a way she hadn't been at nineteen, thrown back into the same room by the inevitability of working in the same field in the same town.

She saw me before I had really decided what to do. Her face slackened in mid-sentence and our eyes met. Even then I could still feel the gentle vibration of her voice when she'd told, in a tiny, drunk whisper, that she liked to choke on it. My cock hardened in sympathetic memory.

She nodded a greeting, bit her lip and didn't smile. She tried to find her way back into the conversation, but I think she knew I couldn't stop watching her. Her motions, now, felt hesitant and suddenly exposed, and eventually, she made some excuse to leave.

Maybe I shouldn't have followed, but it felt like an invitation. At least, it was all the invitation I needed. I saw her heading out the back door, past the bathrooms and onto a dingy back street. An unsavory smell wafted from the trash cans, a dizzying contrast to the glittering facade on the other side.

"You got a cigarette?" she asked. She wasn't looking at me; she was leaning against the brick wall, looking up at the night sky. People always talk about light pollution in the big cities, but there were a ton of stars, like freckles in a summer face.

"You smoke?"

"No." She held out her hand anyway. I jumped off the step into the back street and then patted down my coat until I unearthed an old and crumpled pack.

"I didn't think you would remember me." She fished for a smoke and then rolled it between her fingers, stared at the filter and the stuffed tobacco on the other side. Her voice was deeper than I remembered, just a little lower in volume.

"Gemma," I said, trying to grasp for proof. But all I could think of in that moment was her job and the way she liked to be fucked. I didn't say either out loud, but her name at least made her look over. There was a ghost of a smile on her face, but maybe it came from the stars.

"I guess you don't remember me too fondly." I don't know why I said it. A shadow crossed her face, and I wondered just how badly I'd behaved that night. My memory got a bit woozy after a third glass of wine.

"What do you want, Logan?"

Straight and to the point. Raw. No sugar on top. I licked my lips, handed her my lighter. She stuck the cigarette between her fingers, popped a light, then watched it fade. Then she did it again. I watched her hands, those beautiful hands.

"Let's go somewhere."

I almost wanted to laugh at the speed at which she turned to me, the expression on her face. She snorted, rubbed her face and finally lit her cigarette. She blew on the flame, though, just watched the smoke escape, a strange smile on her face.

"That's funny."

I didn't know what to say. That was funny, too. I was supposed to be eloquent; I'm known for it in interviews. My few loyal fans love it in my songs. But she brought me up short.

"Shouldn't you ask me if I have a partner before you waste any time out here?"

I cringed. Visibly, I think, because she seemed to stand a little taller in response. I wondered how many years she had held on to those words. A few minutes earlier, I would have scoffed, I think, at the idea that I hurt her back then. It was just one night. I never even saw her naked. But I saw it in her face then.

I leaned against the wall next to her and lit a cigarette of my own. Unlike Gemma, I brought it to my mouth though, and sucked the stinging smoke into my lungs. It felt good. I stared at the one in her hand, the glowing point, the elegant fingers, turning and turning it to keep the flame alive.

"Come on. Let's go somewhere." I scratched my head, felt my head swimming a little, and kicked a stone across the back street. "Please?"

She threw me this weird, contemptuous, almost pitying gaze, but then, just when I was ready to give up, she shrugged and nodded. She was the one who walked ahead, wound her way gracefully between trash cans and soaked cardboard boxes. I trotted behind, watched her broad shoulders, the oddly angular curves that had driven me to such curiosity all those years ago. I hadn't changed. I still wanted to see her naked. But she had liked me, back then, and her eyes had shone with curiosity and interest. They didn't now. There was something else, something I had no access to.

"So where do you want to go?"

I nodded away from the clubs, all with bright and flashing neon signs. I wanted to say something, but I didn't know where to start. Hell, I hardly knew why I wanted to be alone with her in the first place, or where we were going—just that it was imperative for me to try. I had a vague idea of taking her down to the river, but then she stopped me a few minutes on.

"Here," she said. It was the entry to a tiny park, a playground and some trees, and she sat on one of the swings. Her shoes crunched on the dirty sand.

She was the one who found words first. I guess that made her braver than me, or smarter, and definitely more beautiful with her skin almost translucent in the moonlight.

"It was stupid. You hurt me. I mean, I get that it's stupid. I was just some girl you wanted to pick up, nothing happened. The end. But it hurt."

I pulled out a fresh cigarette. I don't know why I offered her one, too, but she seemed to enjoy watching them burn, and she fished one out as well. The light struck bright against the darkness around us.

"It's not stupid."

She shrugged, managed a pitying smile.

"I kept seeing your face everywhere. Your name. It's like they played your songs on a loop on the radio then. For years I didn't get it. It should have been nothing."

"Yeah. Should have been. Wasn't."

She shook her head in agreement. It wasn't nothing. I sat down on the other swing and tried to make sense of the ache in my chest.

"I think...I think I wanted you to save me so badly." I looked up, tried to see her face in the shadows. Her voice was raspy and frail. "I was so, so unhappy. I didn't know it, really, but I was. And then you came, and you were bright and strange and I wanted to crawl inside of you and live a fuller life. I wanted you to save me."

I rubbed my face. It was a shock when I felt moisture in the corner of my eye and I looked away, sucked smoke deep into my lungs.

"I didn't know."

"Yeah." She turned toward me, smiled in the dark. "I know. Neither did I. It was good. That you didn't know, I mean. It meant I had to save myself. Took me a while, but you gotta learn sometime, right?"

I nodded, although I wasn't sure I had a right to. I grasped the chain of her swing and pulled her closer; our feet bumped against each other and she leaned her cheek against my knuckles. I don't know how she did it, the brutal honesty, stripping down walls like clothes. I remembered how she'd done the same all those years ago, and how powerful it was then, too. I couldn't do that.

I wanted to say that I was sorry. That the only reason I acted the way I did was because something about her had gotten inside of me so deep that it left a gouging hole when I realized she couldn't be mine. And I felt betrayed, like she'd wormed herself inside just to go away again, that glimmer of something that could be more than fucking, more than searching, more than flitting from girl to girl. And I wanted to say that I hadn't known any of that two minutes ago.

I couldn't say it, though. I blamed being a man, or my upbringing, but the truth was that I was never as brave as Gemma.

"Strange isn't it?" she said after a long, oddly comfortable silence, broken only by the squeaking of the swings. "It's been so long. And...I kind of hated you for most of the time. But it feels like...I still know you. The way it felt back then. Like..."

"Like we're picking up where we left off."

"Yeah." She was almost all voice now, just a shadow in the dark, a warm cheek against my hand. "Something like that."

"I wouldn't care this time."

I felt her cheekbone move over my knuckles, the brush of her nose.

"About what?" she asked.

"Whether you're with someone." I looked down at my dark feet in the sand. My hand around the chain of her swing tightened once, then I lifted a finger off it, touched my knuckle to her face. It was softer than I thought it would be. Warmer, too, cheeks like a flower petal furnace. "I don't know if that's even more douchey, and it's a fucked-up way to say I'm sorry, but I just don't care. This time, I would save you."

There are things you only understand by saying them out loud, truths that have to be verbalized to become truths. This one hurt, it hurt like a tattoo. It hurt like frozen flesh thawing.

Her lips touched the back of my hand. I heard the quiet plop and smack of a kiss, felt the heat of her breath. She sniffed, and then blindly we were on our feet, and her lips found mine. Her cheeks were wet and so were mine, but it didn't matter in the dark. Like secrets whispered in vacuum. Like a tree that falls in the woods.

She was my height. Her lips lay on mine, no stretching or stooping, no tension at all. They were wet with tears and shivered, hummed, vibrated against mine. They tasted like salt. Mine or hers, I didn't know.

I was a different person in the dark.

"Maybe I'm going to save you this time," she whispered and her fingers traced my face; they rubbed against the stubble on my jaw, and down my neck. When she held on to my shirt, I touched her arm. I felt hard muscle under her dress, hard muscle under soft skin.

I remembered her eyes, that bright aquamarine. I could see them, a memory that reached out across the years. She said it was the color of the sea, the color of A minor. I should have corrected her; I should have told her that everything about her was a major chord.

"Come on," she said, and took my hand, squeezed it tight. She knew where to go now, and I knew it, too.

Her apartment was just like her: spacious and intriguing. No frills or clutter. Guitars lined the exposed brick wall to her bedroom. I held on to her hand, pulled her back to me and kissed her against that wall between two Fenders.

She was stronger than me, I think. But she yielded so easily. She cupped my face while I pulled her dress up over her hip. I traced the elastic of her panties through her tights. Her ass was firm and soft, all at once, like everything about her.

She was dizzyingly surreal, and finally in my arms.

"You have to go slow," she whispered, pushing her thumb over my lips before I could say anything. Her eyes glowed blue in the hallway light that glittered on the polished guitars. "You have to mean it."

A strand of her hair stuck to the exposed brick. She bit her lip, then pushed her thumb past mine. Our eyes locked, and I swirled my tongue around her intrusion. She tasted like salt and smoke.

"You're dangerous, you know?"

I don't know how she did that, how she could look smaller with just a sentence, just a flick of her eyelids. My grip on her ass hardened and I felt my knuckles bruise against the brick behind her.

"I don't know anyone who can hurt me like you could. That's why I want you so bad. That's why..." She shook her head, pulled her thumb from my mouth and looked at the gloss of my saliva. "Nobody makes me feel weak like you do."

I kissed the palm of her hand, her cheek, her nose.

"I know..." I knew from stinging eyes and a dumbstruck tongue. I knew from the moisture on my cheeks, from an outburst of pointless, vicious anger five years ago. I knew. And then I knew where the pain came from, the biting gnawing feeling in my chest that had followed us around all night.

It was five lost years. Five years in which I could have been happy. Five years unraveling and catching up. I kissed her again, and time spun around us, speeding up and slowing down like a crazy carousel ride.

Her bed was a vast sprawl of blankets. I laid her down, dressed like she was, and she smiled up at me. She hadn't turned on the lights but a streetlamp shed an orange glow that made her eyes look almost green.

I pulled off my jacket; the leather squeaked in the silence. Maybe for the first time in my life, I had an inkling that I could wait, that I could kick off my shoes, climb in bed with her and hold her until we fell asleep. I saw myself making breakfast in the morning. I'd pick a guitar from the wall, and we'd write something together the way she talked about five years ago. And I would sleep with her only once she knew that I meant it this time. That, no matter my reputation, no matter what I did that night we met, no matter all of it: I meant it this time.

I liked myself in that vision. But I think she already knew, somehow.

She brushed her shoes off with her toes, and then lifted her foot into my hands. Her heel rested against my stomach. I touched her calf, and her arches. I counted her toes under the dark tights. I liked her legs, liked the sheer length, the stability. She could have sent me sprawling on the floor with just one good push, but she didn't. Her leg was soft and pliable under my hands. The contrast made my cock ache.

She wriggled her toes under my shirt. There they rested, hot against my stomach.

"Take it off?" It was a sweet sound, half question, half command. I felt light as air, smiled down at her and my shirt joined my jacket on a chair. I saw her chest expand as her eyes roamed my torso, saw her tongue flicker over her bottom lip.

It's a powerful drug, being wanted. I knew that too well, maybe; I was an addict by all accounts. But my usual hits didn't compare to being wanted by Gemma.

I stepped between her legs, rested my knee on the side of the bed. She lifted her ass for me so that I could pull her tights and panties out from beneath her dress. I painted a line of kisses down her leg as I exposed her skin. Slowly.

It was the sweet smell of her cunt, I think, that made me drop to the floor next to her tights, hollow and still warm like the abandoned skin of a snake. My eyes sought hers for approval, maybe, or just connection; something in me jumped at her surprise, at the shock of vulnerability. I smiled against her thigh. Kissed that pale strip of skin.

Her legs closed behind my neck even before I reached her cunt. It was nestled so prettily in the dark, but I pried her legs apart, grinning up at her. I wanted to see, I wanted to peel her open, taste every part of her. I liked her surprise, too. And I savored it like the first taste of her clit, like her moan when I bit her labia, when I pushed two fingers inside her and held her down so I could keep sucking her clit with any amount of traction.

It was dark between her legs, and warm. It was salty and alive with her wriggling, writhing body. She was still half dressed when she came the first time, and so was I. Her cunt clenched around my fingers hard and fast, like her hands around my hair.

She held on to me long after she cried out my name. I rested my cheek against her thigh, breathed her in, smiled at the way her fingers mirrored the rhythm of her cunt.

That, too, was a new sensation: the desire to be held on to. To be kept and not let go.

I kissed her slit, carefully. She squirmed, whimpered again, and I lifted her legs onto the bed. She looked flushed and happy. She plucked open my jeans, but left me to get rid of them before I joined her in bed.

"You taste like me," she whispered, brushing her fingers along my lips. "Make me taste like you, too?"

I looked up surprised, maybe where I shouldn't have been. That old conversation shot back into my head. She liked to be fucked raw and hard and honest.

I peeled her out of her dress, pulled her to the side of her bed, where I could feed her my cock. She lay on her back, suckled it upside down like a lifeline, like a woman, like the most beautiful thing I'd ever seen. Still glowing from her orgasm, every movement was slow, soft, like a kitten after her nap. From time to time, her hip bucked up in unconscious imitation of her lips around my cock. I squeezed her nipples, hard. And each time her moan sent the shock of vibration through her mouth, I had to close my eyes to stop me from drowning in her vertigo.

I started fucking her mouth when her moans became louder, needier, when she started to seem distracted. Her toes curled inward each time I pushed against her throat, each time she drew a ragged breath. Her hand clenched around my thigh as she choked, but she didn't push me away. That's when I knew. Long before her other hand moved between her legs, before I came on her face and she beamed at me upside down. That's when I knew we understood each other. That no time had passed in five long years, and we were just beginning.

I wanted to write a lifetime of songs about that smile alone.

TRIPLE THREAT

Rachel Kramer Bussel

I used to think I knew everything in my twenties. Now, in my early forties, I can laugh at my younger self, who'd race from bar to bar, bed to bed, living utterly in the moment. I rarely stopped to think what would happen after last call, after the sun came up, or whether all those late nights and flings would catch up with me.

Then I fell for Luke, with his big brain, big body, big dick and the most self-confidence I have ever seen in anyone. He would walk into a room—any room—and be sure that everyone would want to talk to him, if only he gave them the chance, which he did, most nights. He would close out bars, with men and women alike buying him drinks, eager to soak up a few moments of his brain power, of those pale-blue eyes and soft as silk hair—well, maybe that was me. I couldn't get enough of that rumbly voice, and the way everything he said made me look at the world around me in new ways. He made me swoon before he even kissed me, so you can only imagine what he was like in bed.

The only problem? His wife, Yvette, who, despite their open relationship, was with him almost all the time. Often, she hung out in the back of the bar, either flirting on her own or keeping a subtle but firm eye on him. She knew he was the type who couldn't be pinned down, and their open relationship went both ways. They had been together since college and were in their mid-thirties, while I had just turned twenty-two. For a while there, I tried as hard as I could to simply be in the moment, to savor the way his skin felt against mine, the way his fingers or tongue or cock felt as they slammed inside of me, the way he could get me to do almost anything just by asking. I'd strip off my panties in a hotel elevator and let him tie my hands behind my back; I would follow him down dark alleys; once I even gave another guy a blow job while Luke watched. Yes, the guy was hot, but what made my whole body tingle wasn't the man's dick growing bigger in my mouth or his voice growing louder in my ear, it was Luke's eyes glued to what I was doing, the way Luke spoke to me, ordering me to pull down my dress, take out my breasts and let the man come all over me. Call me crazy, but it felt like Luke was coming on me too—and yes, Luke did later that night.

When I was with him, nothing else existed in the world, but I was too young and needy to share him. After six months, I told him I had to go cold turkey. I was starting to obsess just a little too much about what he did with Yvette, about why he even wanted me when he could have her. She would smile at me when we ran into each other, try to make small talk, compliment my shoes, but I'd just want to cry.

Cut to the present. I'm a divorced single mom of an adorable five-year-old daughter. I want for little, having made a killing in the stock market. I have a cordial relationship with my ex-husband, friendly enough that I can call him at the last minute and see if he'll watch Tara. I date, but haven't met anyone in the last three years who really did it for me—to be honest, I haven't met anyone in the last twenty who made me feel anything like Luke.

I had been happy to read that he'd moved to Europe, but now he and Yvette were back in our town, which was big enough that I wouldn't see them every day, but was bound to run into them once in a while. I'd figured after Europe they'd move to New York or San Francisco, somewhere cosmopolitan, where they could get their freak on amongst others who shared their kinks. I had heard enough through the grapevine to know that they were into sex parties, swing clubs, kink—with each other and new partners. What was their secret? How had they stayed together so long? Was the fact that they weren't wedded to monogamy the secret to their success? And, more importantly, was I ready to open myself up to something new?

In my heart of hearts, I couldn't deny it—I still wanted Luke, with every fiber of my being. All I had to do was think about his face, his kiss, and my heart would start pounding and my entire body would get hot. Usually tears would rush to my eyes. No matter what else had happened in the intervening years, he was a part of me. But was I a part of him too? How can you know those things when you haven't spoken to someone in so long? There was a time when it was like we were psychically connected; I would have a dream about him, and he would call. He'd slip away from Yvette and text me something filthy, which usually made me stop whatever I was doing and respond. Even after I got married, there were moments, before I cut him off altogether, where just the sight of his name was enough to make my world stop.

I knew once I had Tara though that something had to change; I couldn't sit around pining for someone I couldn't have, who was already as intimately intertwined with another person as you could get. Where would there ever be room for me? Yet now, maybe there could be. I decided to wait and see what the world had in store for us.

I ran into Yvette at the most mundane location imaginable—not while I was wearing fishnets and heels and showing off my best body part, my cleavage, or even sipping a coffee, smudging my blazing red lipstick against the mug, but at the grocery store, in sweats and a threadbare T-shirt. I had left Tara with a sitter since I'd had to run a few other errands beforehand. Yvette wasn't dressed up either, but somehow her pale-gray off-the-shoulder top, revealing her sleek, tan shoulder, and yoga pants and sneakers looked casual chic on her.

Yvette was the one who noticed me first. She reached up to tap me on the shoulder. "Brandy?" Her voice wasn't wary or shy or nervous, simply inquisitive.

I smiled back—or half smiled, really. "Hey, I heard you guys were back in town."

"We are. Luke's just on the other side picking up some ice cream."

"Oh," I said, unable to even feign eloquence. Luke, the man whose image kept me up at night, who even now could make my pussy throb when I let down my guard, was here, in this store? And his wife, perfect goddess that I had always pictured her to be, was talking to me as if this were any other chance encounter between neighbors?

"Look, Brandy, I just want you to know..." I held my breath. What could she possibly want me to know? "I get it—you and Luke. I get that you have this connection that's all yours. Yes, he still thinks about you—he says your name in his sleep sometimes. You are part of the reason he wanted to come back. He hates that things got so messy and muddled. I love him—always have, always will. I want him to be happy and, well, I just wanted to tell you that I'm not your enemy. Maybe I could even be your friend. The three of us together—

whatever form that takes—we could be a triple threat."

Then she walked away, leaving me standing in front of rows of olives with my jaw hanging open, which is exactly how Luke found me. "Hey," he said. Then he just stood and looked at me until I shivered. I thought of the dress I had worn on our first date, the way his hands had felt wrapped around my waist when he lifted me in the air.

"Hey," I said.

"How've you been?"

"Okay." I wasn't in the mood for small talk, not when I had so little air left. He still had the ability to do that to me. "Yvette said hi too."

"She has nothing but good things to say about you, in case you're wondering. In fact, all those years ago she wanted to get in your pants. If anyone was jealous, it was her."

"Yvette?" I laughed. "That's ridiculous. Anyway, that was such a long time ago."

"But you still feel it, don't you, Brandy?"

"I'd be lying if I said I didn't. I don't want to talk about it in the middle of the grocery store though."

"Let's go somewhere. Anywhere." Thank god he didn't say "just to talk."

"Invite Yvette."

"Are you sure?"

"It's been twenty years; if I can't talk to her by now, I'm really in trouble. I just have to call my sitter."

"I heard you had a kid...congratulations." I didn't ask about the wistful look on his face.

"Thanks, she's great. You talk to Yvette and I'll make my call."

We reconvened a few minutes later outside the store, our hands empty. I had considered a bottle of wine but liquid courage was what I'd used all those years ago to blot out my jealousy.

"This is a crazy idea, but what if we pretend this our first date?" I blurted out. I knew they'd had threesomes aplenty, and so had I, but it was our first time trying something new, older and wiser and more sexually experienced. Much as I had battled with envy, I'd craved what the two of them shared, finding my mind wondering how Luke kissed Yvette, how he fucked her, how he made her come. Always on the heels of those thoughts my selfishness had rushed in, but standing there with the two of them, with nothing to lose after I'd already lost him once, I let the envy pass right by me. In its place was something stronger, headier.

"I'm game," Yvette said quietly, moving forward to kiss me on the cheek. Her lips barely grazed my skin, whisper soft, a hint of something floral, sweet and spicy hitting my nose. My eyes met Luke's over her head. He didn't smile or nod, just stared at me, rock steady. All those years of misspent lust melted away as I pulled her closer. She was small but as my hand pressed against her spine, a core of strength radiated outward.

Luke stepped forward to kiss the side of my neck, the one spot that had always driven me mad back in the day. When Yvette shifted around and kissed the other side of my neck in the corresponding spot, my pussy tightened. Triple threat indeed.

"Your place or ours?" Luke whispered. I laughed at the absurdity of it as Yvette nuzzled up against me. What was it about turning forty that had turned my head so completely around that the woman I had sworn was my enemy was now making me wet? How could it be that the man whose wedding ring she wore was about to fuck both of us and I was giddy with anticipation? Could we have had this all along and I was just too stubborn to entertain the idea?

No matter now. "Yours," I boldly decided. If I got cold feet, I could always leave.

"Yvette will drive." Some things hadn't changed—Luke was

as commanding as ever. "You'll join me in the backseat." I know some women might have bristled at an ex waltzing in and telling them what to do after all that time, but me? I welcomed it. I had been the one telling someone what to do seemingly twenty-four-seven for the last five years; I was ready to do anything he asked.

"How far away do you live?"

"Far enough," he said as he guided me into the backseat. "Show Yvette how pretty those breasts are," he said. "They're going to be in her mouth soon." Other guys over the years had tried to talk dirty to me, but they'd always come up short, stumbling over their words, giggling, or simply not owning them properly. Luke owned everything about what was about to happen—all he had needed was my okay.

I unbuttoned my blouse and peeled down the sheer black mesh, grateful my breasts were still firm, still my favorite body part. "Angle your legs so she can see you," Luke said, and immediately, my knees fell open. This was what it had felt like twenty years ago—daring, reckless, a little crazy and blazingly hot. But this time, there was no sneaking around, no hiding, no guilt. Luke was mine, but he was also Yvette's, and I belonged, right now, to both of them.

As Yvette started the car, Luke hiked up my jean skirt enough to give her a view without showing every bit of me to anyone who might pass by. He pulled aside my panties to show off my wetness. I threw my head back and closed my eyes, holding the seat tight as he pinched my clit. "That's your punishment—the start of it, anyway—for disappearing, Brandy. It killed me to know you wanted nothing to do with me." His words wafted over me as the pain shot from my clit and radiated outward, heating up my core. "You didn't even let me know you were okay after Tara; I had to ask around about you. But I knew you couldn't have changed too much; you'll always be my slut, won't you? I told Yvette that too, told her all about how dirty you are." His fingers were inside me, stretching me, making me clench hard around him. I had dreamed of him taking me like this, in countless positions and scenarios, ones where my whole body was full of him.

"Pull over," I heard as his fingers withdrew. The car immediately turned; I opened my eyes to see we were in an empty parking lot. Yvette stopped the car, took off her seat belt and turned around. Luke planted his fingers in front of her. Instead of diving for them as I would have, she locked eyes on me and slowly stretched out her tongue like a cat, licking my cream from his fingers. He pushed them slowly in and out, fucking her mouth. I let out a loud moan. "Strip," he said. "Both of you."

I started to lift my shirt, but he pulled his fingers from her mouth, reached over me and opened the door. "Out there. You and Yvette need to learn what it means to listen. She didn't believe me either, that both of you could get along. But I always knew; two filthy sluts who can't get enough cock." Was this really happening? The whole day had felt like a dream, so why not go with it? I didn't have to be back home until morning. And even though he was the most sadistic man I had ever met, I trusted Luke to protect us.

I stumbled out of the car and got naked as fast as possible, Yvette right on my heels. "Keep the shoes," Luke said, tossing ours at us. I leaned against the car and slipped back into my flats, admiring Yvette's tall black-and-gold ones. While he got out of the car, she pressed herself against me, her lips once again seeking me out. She clearly knew all of his tricks, because soon it was Yvette squeezing my clit, her small fingers making me quiver so hard I wondered if I could stay upright.

"I know you love sucking cock, Brandy, but I want to see what you do with a mouthful of pussy." Only a man who knew exactly what an oral fixation I had—*have*—could say that with the certainty that I'd do exactly as commanded. He lifted Yvette onto the hood of the car, then guided my face toward her neatly trimmed bush, her lips glistening. I took one long, slow lick along her slit before zeroing in on her clit, but that wasn't what he wanted. He pushed my face deep into her, reminding me of the way he used to wrap his leg around my head to press his cock deeper down my throat.

"Make her come and I'll make you come," he said. He stood behind me, still fully clothed, hopefully blocking us from view. I slid my hands under Yvette's ass and pulled her close. She let me know exactly what she liked, her moans filling the open air as I alternated sucking on her hard clit and sliding my tongue inside her. When Luke spread my asscheeks apart, I really lost it, tonguing her for all I was worth. When he added his tongue to my crack, I went crazy. That was the thing about Luke—he could sound like a mean bastard, spank me until I could barely sit down, but then he would treat me to the most glorious tongue lashing imaginable. I shifted so I could press three fingers inside Yvette while adding more pressure to her clit. Luke fingered me too, while his tongue tormented me.

I was too overwhelmed, not to mention busy, to make noise, but Yvette let us know she was going to come, her sex tightening around my hand. When she sat up and kissed me fiercely, Luke added another finger, and I came too. He pulled out and we leaned against each other, panting. "That was just the start of what I have planned for you girls." I was far from a girl, but maybe that was the point. When I had been a girl, I used to think I knew everything. Now I knew only the here and now. I wasn't looking to tomorrow or forever, wasn't even asking what was next.

I looked from him to her and back. "I'm ready." And I was— nothing threatening about it.

COLLEGE DAYS

Kim Strattford

M ira walked along the path between the administration building and the student union building, where she would meet the latest batch of parents and prospective students for Raynaud College. She nodded to students as she passed, knowing more than a few of them. Raynaud was a small university, liberal in outlook, but picky in who was accepted. The dean liked to say they were one of the mini-ivies, but Mira wasn't sure they really rated that high. Not that she would ever correct him about it.

It was one of the lovely days they got in May, the weather perfect, just before it switched to hot and humid and reminded northern Virginia residents that they did, in fact, live in the South. Mid-Atlantic meant nothing except in the winter, when storms sometimes missed them as if they were under a bubble. Which was fine with her, she had moved to the DC area nearly twenty years ago to get away from the weather in upstate New York.

Well, and to get away from James Clanton. But she wasn't going to think about him.

A resolution that worked great until she walked into the student union building and saw him in the group clustered around Jeannie, one of the student tour guides for the campus visits.

"Shit," Mira muttered and closed her eyes for a moment. What the hell was he doing at Raynaud?

"Here she is," Jeannie said. "Please let me present our head of admissions, Ms. Mira Losacek."

Mira tried to ignore James as she led the group to the small auditorium and watched them take their seats. He was with a young woman who didn't look much like him, being blonde with light eyes—Mira didn't want to stare to see exactly what color—and short. James was graying but most of his hair was full and dark, playing off his dark-brown eyes, and he was taller than she remembered.

Mira forced herself to look away—who cared if his eyes still looked like melted chocolate? Or that his wife must be a knockout judging from his daughter.

His *wife*. Mira had been waiting for him to pop the damn question for three years before she gave up. Since he had an eighteen-year-old daughter, he must have done it as soon as Mira left him—but he had asked someone else.

Mira gave her standard "What we look for in a Raynaud student" speech, then asked for questions. A sea of hands went up. James's hand wasn't one of them.

Good, all the easier to ignore him. She gave herself over to what she was there for, encouraging the students Raynaud would want to apply and doing some advance softening for those who wouldn't get accepted.

When no other hands went up, she smiled, thanked the groups and wished them well on the rest of their tour, and left them in Jeannie's capable hands. She walked out as professionally as she could, trying her best not to look like she was fleeing.

She had gotten out to the exit when she heard his voice, "Mir, wait up."

Taking a deep breath, she turned around, hoping her face didn't betray what she was feeling. Damn it all—why did he have to look so good? "James."

"I was hoping I'd see you."

"Don't know why." She made her tone as icy as it could go. Buffalo icy. Winds blowing off the Lakes icy.

He didn't look perturbed. "My ex-wife wanted to be the one to take Jaime to all the schools, but this one I managed to snag. Wonder why that is?" His grin was the same as she remembered, lighting up his face, making those chocolate eyes crinkle.

"*Ex*-wife?"

His grin grew wider. "Caught that, did you?"

She shrugged. "Just making conversation."

His gaze seemed to drop to her fingers. "No rings. Does that mean you're not married?"

"Guess so." She turned.

He closed the gap between them, reached past her and held the door shut.

"Students may want in, you idiot."

Laughing, he let go of the door. "Have dinner with me tonight."

"With you and Jaime?"

"Nope. She's being wined and dined—well, I hope not wined, actually—by the women's field hockey team. She's really good."

Mira found herself smiling and tried to dial it back, with no luck. "We have a decent team. Never going to make the Olympics or anything, but good."

"Yeah, she's really good but not stellar. Her expectations are set right, I think." He eased Mira out of the way of some students, moving her the way he used to, his hand falling low on her back. She had thought it was a possessive thing, when she'd still believed he wanted to keep her. "Dinner? Please?"

"I'm seeing someone."

"Liar."

She knew she was glaring.

"You have a tell when you lie. You always have and I've never told you that. And I don't plan on telling you what it is now, but you have it, and you just did it when you said you were seeing someone." His smile was one sided, slipping up into a grin of triumph. "You're mad at me still? That's okay. Just have dinner with me."

Her brain said to say no. Her brain said to walk away without answering: that would teach him. Her brain said to— "Fine. Yes. Shut up."

He seemed to like the answer, even with the "shut up" part thrown in. "We're staying at the University Motel. Or I can come to you?"

"I'll pick you up." He had always driven when they'd been together; her driving would make him crazy. She smiled a little at the thought.

"Great. Say, seven?"

"Fine." She pushed him away. "Go find your group. I'm not going to entertain you the rest of the day if you lose them."

"They were on bathroom break when I made my run for it." He leaned in, kissed her on the cheek, and murmured, "You look fabulous, by the way," and then he was gone, striding across the student union as if he owned it.

She hated that she watched him until he disappeared into the auditorium.

She arrived at his motel a little after seven and picked up the house phone, waiting as she was connected to his room. No one answered. She hung up the phone, frowning, and then felt the hackles-rising feeling she occasionally got when she was the object of scrutiny.

She turned and saw him sitting in the bar across the lobby, a lazy smile on his face. He lifted his glass to her, and she walked over.

"You thought I'd bailed?" He motioned the bartender over. "You still drink daiquiris?"

"No, I'll have a club soda."

"You laying off booze for a reason?"

"Yes, I'm driving."

He motioned for her to sit next to him. "Why don't we eat here?"

"Why?"

"Because I'm afraid you're going to get pissed off at me at some point and strand me in the middle of a town I don't know. This way, I have a short walk."

She laughed despite herself. "Are you planning on pissing me off?"

"No, but the possibility is there."

She conceded the point with an eye roll and stopped the bartender as she sat. "Can you put some scotch in that?"

"Wow, scotch and soda. Aren't you all grown up?"

"I damn well better be after all these years." She turned to look at him. "So, I checked Jaime's file. She may not be stellar in field hockey but her grades and extracurriculars are up there."

His smile was easy and sweet. "She's a great kid. I thought when her mom and I divorced that we would ruin her, but she's dealt with it better than Linda or I have."

"When did you divorce?"

"About four years ago." He sipped his drink—scotch also from the look of it. "We drifted apart. Or maybe we didn't drift at all. Maybe we just bored each other." He sighed and it had the sound of a longstanding frustration, as if he wished he really did know why he and this Linda had broken up.

"People change." She sipped her drink, reminding herself to go easy, no matter how much she wanted to throw it back and feel the rush of calm—why was she so nervous? She had left him, not the other way around.

"I should have changed."

"For her, you mean?"

He shook his head. "For you. Before you left me, you wanted to get married and I..." He closed his eyes for a moment, then opened them and studied her, his gaze so appraising she wasn't sure what he was looking for. "I loved you so much. I never loved Linda that way."

"Didn't stop you from proposing to her. So I guess it pays to be her." She played with the ice in her glass, tipping the glass slightly back and forth, until he stopped her.

"I'm serious. I never loved her—never loved anyone—the way I loved you." He began to move his finger over her hand, tracing patterns the way he'd used to in bed. "I can't regret Linda because together we have Jaime, and I love her more than anything. So maybe in that sense it was meant to be. But not forever, you know? Not the love of my life."

She eased her hand out from under his, tried not to let him see how much his touch had moved her. "I have always thought the love of your life was you."

He surprised her by laughing out loud. "You never would have said that before."

"I sure wouldn't have." She laughed softly. "Life is a great teacher. So is loss. Why mince words?"

"Why indeed. In the spirit of not mincing words, I want you to know something. I came here to get you back."

She let her eyebrows rise. "What?"

"That was pretty basic English, but if I really need to rephrase it, I will."

"Maybe 'why' is the better question."

"Because I was an idiot."

"Well on that you'll get no argument from me." She leaned against the back of the bar stool. "You really thought one trip here, one short little meeting, maybe dinner, and we would be all hot and heavy again?"

He smiled and looked pointedly at the hand he had been tracing his nonsense symbols on. "You liked having me touch you. Just now and earlier, in the student union, when I did this." He slid his hand between her and the stool, letting it settle on the small of her back, radiating an astonishing amount of heat—it wasn't right that he could still do this to her.

She'd had other men since she left him. Plenty of them. Why in the hell had none of them moved her the way he did?

She leaned forward, trying to break the connection, but he followed her, his hand never leaving her back.

She felt the tingle in her belly she'd always felt when she was around him, knew he would find her wet and ready if they went up to his room and—

Shit. Shit, shit, shit, shit.

"Why would I want to get back with you?" Good. Turn this back on him—she shouldn't be thinking about how her belly felt like butterflies had taken up residence in it, or that she wanted him to lean her over the bar and—

"Because you love me."

"I don't love your ego."

He laughed. "You love that I keep you on your toes. You always have. I love that, too."

She reached behind her and grabbed his hand, pulling it off her back. "Yes, you loved it so much you wouldn't put a ring on it."

"You scared the crap out of me, Mir. I got lost in you. Nothing else mattered when we were together."

"Those are arguments for marrying someone, not against. Tell me something that actually makes sense."

He grabbed his glass, sipped his drink almost angrily, then put it back with what looked like great care. "I had plans. I had ambition. I was afraid if I was with you, I would forget them."

"Well, I hope your plans and ambition kept you warm."

"They did. At first. I was important—still am, I suppose. I married a woman who would never make me question what was the most important thing in my life: my work."

"You know, when men have midlife crises like this, they usually go for someone really young and flashy."

"Linda was flashy. Where do you think Jaime gets her looks from? But she gets her brains from me. She and her mom don't have much to talk about because Jaime tends to care about more than the latest gossip rags." He met Mira's eyes. "She's like us that way. Smart. Deep."

"Wow, aren't we wonderful?" The words didn't come out as snotty as she meant them to because she was liking what he was saying. She was liking it way too much.

"I have an opportunity for a job in Maryland. It's a lateral assignment, and that's okay because I'm ready to quit pushing so hard. But I won't take it if you don't want me to." He met her eyes, stilled fingers she hadn't realized she was drumming on the bar. "Mir, tell me what you want."

"It's been twenty years, James."

"It's been nineteen years and five months." He leaned in. "And four days. And I've missed you every single bit of that time."

She wasn't sure what to say; she *always* knew what to say.

"Mir, do you want me here?"

"I hated you." The words came out almost strangled; it was a truth she'd held back for so long. Hate was counterproductive. Hate made you live in the past and she had moved on. She had forgotten him.

Only she hadn't. Not the way he smiled, or the way his eyes crinkled, even if they crinkled more than before. The way his hand felt on hers. The way his lips would feel.

He sighed. "I hated myself more than a little, too. It just took me a long time to realize that I had made the wrong thing a priority. Even after I left Linda, I wanted to believe that my job, doing what felt good, what made me *seem* important, was more vital than finding you and letting you know how I felt."

"It's probably good you did. Four years ago I really was seeing someone."

"You left him, too, huh?"

She nodded. "After he asked me to marry him and I couldn't say yes."

"Because of me."

She hated that he didn't even make it a question. She hated that he was right. She hated what that said about her, the kind of woman who could never move on. "Because of me," she finally said. And wasn't that the truth, after all? She was the one who had never moved on even though she had moved away. She was the one who had never forgotten him.

Or maybe...she wasn't. Maybe he was telling the truth: he had thought about her all this time.

She studied him. "You're important—you're fixed fine for money, I take it?"

He nodded.

"Then the drink's on you." She stood up.

"What are you doing?"

"I'm leaving." She smiled, and for once the smile didn't feel full of old anger and pain and longing. "What are you doing?"

"You want me to come with you?" He looked seriously confused at this point. "I need you to tell me what you want."

"No, you don't. Move here if you want to see how I feel.

Don't, if you need a sure thing. Because I'm not going to be that. Not after twenty years apart." She leaned in and kissed his cheek the way he had done to her earlier. "You look fabulous, too, by the way."

Then she pulled away, turned on her heel, and went home.

She didn't hear from him that night, or in the weeks that followed, so she pushed the brief sharp pain away and went back to her life. One day she saw Jaime on campus and smiled at the girl but didn't stop to talk, and Jaime didn't seem to know Mira was anyone that might have been important to her.

She pushed thoughts of James out of her mind and stayed in her office the rest of the day, letting work divert her, until she packed it in and drove home.

As she pulled into her driveway, she saw James sitting on her front step, kicked back, a reader in his hand. He closed it and smiled at her, then stood up.

She got out of the car and walked to him.

"So I moved." He pointed at a car parked across the streets. "Commuting to Maryland from Virginia is a bitch."

"You could have lived in Maryland, Mister 'I'm so much smarter than my ex.'"

He laughed. "But I wanted to be close to Jaime." He drew her in. "And to you."

"I've gotten married. Sorry." She tried to keep a straight face and failed.

"Where is your new groom? I'll fight him for you."

She let him draw her up the stairs, smiled as he took the key from her and opened the door. "Mr. Traditionalist?"

"I want to stake my claim for this mythical rival."

She closed the door and leaned against it. "Unfortunately for me, you have no rival."

He moved closer. "No?"

"Nope." She felt a lightness she didn't expect, a...happiness she'd given up on at some point.

He had moved here not knowing if she'd take him back. As gestures went, that was big. Even if his daughter was here, too. It still counted for a hell of a lot.

"Do you wish you didn't love me?" He drew her jacket off, took her purse and put it on the table near the door.

"My answer tonight might be different than my answer a few weeks ago."

He reached behind her and locked the door. "Good." He began to unbutton her blouse.

She stopped him. "I'm older."

"So am I, toots. Now, move those hands and let me look at you."

She let her hands fall, and he made short work of the buttons and pushed her blouse off. Reaching around her, he unhooked her bra and let it fall too. Then he just stared.

"I thought I had made you better in my mind, you know? But I didn't." He unfastened her pants, and let them pool, eased off her panties and knelt down, his tongue finding her clit.

"You haven't even kissed me, James." The last part came out a little breathy since he was doing amazing things where he was using his mouth.

"You want me to stop?" he asked, as he pulled away.

"I'm an idiot. Forget I said anything."

He laughed and went back to work, his tongue sliding around and then over her clit, his fingers kneading her rear, and then he moved them around and up, one, then two, then—

Her legs didn't want to support her, so she slid down, and he eased her back, her clothing partially protecting her from the hard tile of her entryway. She forgot about how cold the floor was as he kept licking and sucking and then she was gone, calling out loudly, suddenly glad she didn't share any walls in this house.

He kissed his way up her body, stopping at her breasts, taking first one nipple, then the other in his mouth, going back and forth, murmuring how he'd missed his girls. When he finally found her mouth, she was feeling the cold easing through her clothing.

He pulled away and said, "Please, god, tell me you have a bed. I'm too old for this."

Laughing, she nodded, and they helped each other up, and he followed her to her bedroom.

He nodded to the bed. "Lie down."

"But you're fully dressed. And I've done very little work here."

"You did the heavy lifting when you left me. Now it's my turn to put in a little effort."

"I think I love that thought." She lay back on the bed, resting on her elbows as she watched him take off his clothes.

"You didn't want me to make this sexy, did you?"

She laughed and shook her head.

"Good. Because I'm pretty sure that'll be your department next time we do this."

"Oh, you want a striptease, do you?"

"I'm a guy. You're the love of my life who is still so damn sexy it hurts. The question is ludicrous." He walked over to her and smiled as she reached out for his cock, as she played with it, making it harder than it already was. "I want a lot of stripteases from you, woman."

"Maybe. If you're lucky." She looked up at him as she played. "I've always loved your cock."

"Hopefully not *just* my cock. I have some skill using it."

"Been a while. Not sure I'll enjoy you." Although if the way he'd gone down on her was any indication...

With a very sweet smile, he eased her hands off him. "Well, let's see, shall we?"

"I was going to give him a kiss."

"Give him a kiss later. He loves your kisses, but right now he wants to be inside you—and so do I." His grin was goofy. "Both of us want you."

"A ménage à trois?"

"I guess so."

As she lay back, he moved over her, kissing her gently, then with more urgency, his tongue hard against hers. She reached down and played with him as he moved into position, then she let go as he pushed into her. She moaned at the feeling of being with him again—of coming home.

"Don't move, don't move," he said, and it sounded like a prayer. "I want you so much..."

He closed his eyes and she wondered which ritual he used to stave off coming, if he still tried to remember the periodic table like he had when they'd first been together. Whatever he did now, it seemed to work, because he opened his eyes and gave her a satisfied smile, then began to move, dipping in, then out, slowly at first, then with greater force.

"I remember you liking it this way." He seemed to be holding back.

"You remember me liking it even rougher than this. That hasn't changed." Even if she'd only told one of the lovers she'd had since James about that preference. Then he had taken it too far the first time and hadn't taken it far enough the next.

James knew exactly how far to take it.

She felt another orgasm building, and by the way his smile changed could tell he knew she was close.

"Touch yourself," he said, watching as she did what he wanted, and then he began to thrust faster, and she felt herself going, falling down and down, landing softly and to the sound of him saying, "I love you, Mir," as he came.

He collapsed against her and she wrapped her legs around

him and held him tightly, as if he might disappear, a figment of her imagination, only here for the moment.

"I'm not going anywhere, sweetheart." He rolled off her and pulled her to him, kissing her softly as she nuzzled against him. "And neither are you. Not for the rest of the night. Or the night after that. Or the night after that. Or…"

"What if I get bored?" she asked, with a laugh.

He reached down and teased her clit; she was so sensitive it almost hurt, and she moaned against his neck. "Somehow, I don't think that will be a problem."

She smiled as he stroked her back. "Somehow, I don't think it will be either."

A FEW
GRAY HAIRS

H. Keyes

Autumn had finally killed off the dreaded humidity of Tokyo's infamous summers and left in its wake a fragrant, mild stretch of weather that rivaled anything that spring and its ubiquitous cherry blossoms could offer. It would soon be time for the Christmas illuminations to be put up and the city would become as crowded during the week as on the weekends, but that was how it had always been. Sarah Blevins hefted her purse up onto her shoulder and entered the small shopping arcade; similarly she had had no expectations of change when she'd started out that morning and indeed was quite comfortable with the status quo given all that had happened.

Weaving her way between the rows of books, Sarah lost herself in the musty smell of used novels and took her time searching for what she wanted in the unusually empty shop. She pulled down various texts on European textiles and traditional Japanese *kanzashi* designs, some written in Japanese, others in English. Formerly a resident of Wales, Sarah had moved to Japan in her early twenties—one of those gap years that turned into a gap decade, and then ultimately a change in citizenship. Living as an expat in Japan had certainly improved her language skills, but if she wanted to keep up with the fast-paced world of accessories design, especially as she had just celebrated her thirty-fifth birthday, she needed to be on top of her game in all areas. That morning had been spent at an interview for a small fashion magazine and accordingly Sarah was dressed in one of her favorite outfits—a black polka-dot-print wrap dress and a custom-printed denim jacket, all of her own design. She'd had pictures taken from every angle, compliments thrown her way and a business card with a cell phone number from the cameraman's assistant. She felt confident and wanted to spend the day amongst humanity—maybe she would even call that number. It was finally cool enough after the unrelenting heat of Tokyo's summer for her to dress in more than one flimsy layer and Sarah was enjoying the lighthearted atmosphere. This day seemed to be promising; in fact, she felt younger and more carefree than she had in years.

She grabbed a couple more texts and then headed off toward the coffee table books—she couldn't spend all her time studying, she reasoned, and soon got lost in photos of gorgeous snow-covered temples and rows of women in kimono dress. She added a book on traditional tattoos to her pile and decided against one on African landscapes, and then against one of the textile books she'd picked up earlier. Sarah made her way back across the shop with her arms overflowing with books, all great bargains and very nearly all unnecessary purchases in the making. She returned a book to the shelf, lingered over another one that caught her eye and, as she perused the first few pages, was suddenly aware of someone standing just behind her.

"Oh, I'm so sorry," she began, feeling a bit rude for having blocked the aisle given how tiny the shop was in the first place, then stopped when she realized *who* it was.

Seichi Sugimoto, a fellow designer and sometime musician, was tanned, dark haired and well muscled; he was wearing a fashionably tailored black shirt and a thin leather jacket with jeans that left little to the imagination. He smiled at her, as charming and irresistible as he had been when they first met.

It was his sense of style and the strange coincidence of them both wearing the same necklace that had attracted Sarah to him a little over six years ago when he had sent her a very charming message on a dating website. He was five years older than her, had lived a very fast-paced life and was looking for a partner— someone that would be his equal, his match as he had termed it. They had met shortly after that initial message and had become fast friends—they'd complemented one another well, a fact that Seichi had often commented on. He'd loved her style, her taste in music, art, motorcycles—it was as if they had known one another forever, or so he'd said. As their relationship grew, they'd come to rely on each other's advice in numerous ways— and despite living in different halves of the country, they had made time for each other. Once a month they spent a weekend together, at the very least.

Until five years ago, that is. Five years ago, the daily text messages had stopped, the phone calls and planned weeklong *are-we-going-to-finally-sleep-together?* visit abruptly cancelled. Sarah was beyond perplexed; at first she'd assumed he was just busy—his designs had been picked up by a fairly well-known brand and he had to focus on that, he was living in another city still and all the other excuses she could imagine. At her weakest, she had even managed to wonder if there hadn't been some sort of accident: was Seichi lying in a coma somewhere, unable to move, much less operate a cell phone? She'd confessed all of this to her friends and in return had been given a copy of the book *He's Just Not That Into You*, which was now dog-eared and heavily highlighted. That book had hit all the marks and left her both ashamed and embarrassed. Sarah had learned her lesson; she had promised herself that she'd get on with her life and had done her absolute best to do just that. She'd gone back to college part-time, added various licenses and certificates in metalworking, jewelry design and marketing to her résumé and, once she had finally worked up the nerve, had started her own Internet shop. She was moderately successful, well-known in the subcultures that she belonged to and lived a reasonably comfortable, if single, life.

There hadn't been a man since Seichi who had understood her or her need to create, and she found it was more often than not far easier to be single that it was to try and adapt herself to someone else, even if it made for a lonely life. She took comfort in the idea that, perhaps in a hundred years, she would be remembered for her work at least.

"Sarah, I thought it was you. I can't believe it though, what are the odds?"

"Seichi! It really is you. It's been so long." Her voice was strange to her ears, strangled with shock and some unnamed emotion. He looked just as gorgeous as the last time she'd seen him despite the extra laughter lines.

"Too long." Seichi smiled and took a step toward her, giving her a friendly, if initially awkward, hug. The hug very quickly went from one-sided and awkward to warm and somehow frantic; Sarah's mind raced, her stack of books tumbled forgotten to the floor as tears pricked at her eyes. *Damn, he smells good... No! You're supposed to hate him for abandoning you, him and his stupid strong arms and good-smelling skin and... Oh fuck it. This feels too good to stop.*

Sarah turned her head and Seichi's mouth went to her throat, leaving a trail of kisses as he pushed her against the nearest bookshelf—a move that killed the mood unfortunately. They were in a bookstore, a very public place doubtlessly filled with security cameras, possibly being watched at that very moment and...they pulled apart. Seichi whispered in her ear, his voice thick with lust and something like desperation, "Please Sarah, come with me. I need to talk to you. Please."

She didn't want to follow him, to give in so willingly to him, not after how much his disappearing act had hurt. The fact that he picked up her books and carried them to the register for her, waited politely as she paid and walked away from the register didn't escape her notice either. It was unlike him to be that patient, to walk next to her instead of going about at his own pace. Perhaps he *had* been in a coma, she thought, and awoke more humble than before. He looked different, acted more mature than he had been five years ago, and yet when she saw their reflection in the mirrored windows of a shop, they looked as though they had coordinated their outfits that morning. She reached up to brush her bangs into a better shape and hiked her shoulder bag up once more. *This is maddening*, she thought as she turned to look at him.

He smiled as they fell in step, the crisp autumn air refreshing and clean. Sarah was silent, waiting expectantly for something, anything to be said. He held out a hand and automatically she handed over her parcel, then his arm wrapped around her shoulders affectionately, the contact both warming and twisting her heartstrings. It was as if they had never been apart—their actions were familiar and almost predictable. It was mind-boggling and Sarah found herself wondering whether or not she should just take off running down the streets, books and appearances be damned.

The fact that the bookstore was in one of the most fashionable districts of Tokyo hadn't escaped her, but who could expect to run into someone from out of town that they hadn't seen in five years in a half-empty bookstore in a place like that? *Maybe it wasn't some freak coincidence, you know, maybe it's one of those butterfly-flapping-causes-a-typhoon kind of things*, the hopeful side of her mind supplied.

Abruptly he stopped outside a small, freshly painted boutique, newspaper still blocking the interior of the shop from the very fashion-forward public. Seichi brought out a key ring and unlocked the door, holding it open for her as her mind raced. When she didn't move, he addressed her in an unusually tender tone. "Sarah, please come inside and hear me out. I want to explain this all to you, just...please?" he pleaded, yet another thing she had never expected him to do.

"Seichi, I think I...well, fine." The earlier tears threatened to overflow as her indignation battled the spark of hope that his hug had inspired in her. She walked into the foyer and looked around—the shop was obviously on the verge of opening. After a brief silence, he spoke again.

"Welcome to my shop," he said, spreading his hands and smiling apologetically. "This is why I...well...why I was kept away from you for so long."

There were rows of shelves and racks full of clothing, boxes littered the floor and a mixed punk rock CD that she recognized as being from his car played in the sound system hidden in the boldly painted walls. He gestured for her to take a seat on a very gorgeous, obviously expensive sofa near the changing rooms. She put her purse down next to her and sank into the plush burgundy fabric as he took a seat opposite her on the solid wood coffee table. He put a hand on her knee and looked her in the eyes, forcing her to confront the situation instead of mentally running away from it.

"I'm so sorry, Sarah, for leaving you like that, I really am. Everything suddenly took off and, I know this isn't any kind of excuse, but I never wanted to lose you. I had to sell my place, got sent overseas and...well, just a lot of things that I couldn't really control, you know?"

Sarah shifted halfheartedly; the warmth from his hand both delighted and pissed her off. She spoke up before he could continue, her tone betraying her hurt and anger.

"In five years, you couldn't find a minute, not a single minute to send me a text message to tell me that you were okay, that you were even alive? You could have told me that at the very least—I even wondered if you'd been in an accident or something!" Tears overran her eyes and she swallowed hard, pointedly looking at him; she got the reply that she'd secretly hoped for.

He cleared his throat and nodded his head; tears had filled and reddened his eyes, as well. He coughed, clearing his throat before he spoke. "I know I screwed up, I know I did Sarah, and...I know that sorry isn't enough, but I am, I really am. Can you...do you even want to forgive me? I...can't say anything in my defense other than that I...I still have feelings for you—I always did. I...I think love you, Sarah."

Those ridiculous tears ran down her cheeks in rivers, as they did down his, and she tried to ignore them, to recall what that book had said, but it was to no avail. His honest confession was breaking her up and she felt herself thawing, opening up to him before her brain had actually decided that he was forgiven. Her heart was set on its own course, it seemed.

"Damn you, I tried to hate you, you know. I tried so hard to hate you Seichi, to make you into a villain." She shook her head, trying to make sense of it all before she lost her nerve. "But I have to know: were you honestly going to ever contact me again if we hadn't run into one another today?" Sarah asked; she had to get it all out of her system or else she wouldn't be able to live with herself.

He looked into her eyes, as if hoping to understand just where he stood. "I did all of this, here in Tokyo, hoping that...well, that we could be together, eventually. I tried calling you once I had secured the lease and everything—but your number was different and I figured you'd gotten married or...I don't know, that you had found someone better than me." He paused, and swallowed hard. "If you won't have me...how am I ever going to find someone like you, Sarah?"

Sarah smiled and placed her hand on the cheek she'd wanted to slap so many times before in the last few years. "You can't, Seichi. You won't get another chance, you know. It's now or nothing."

She kissed him softly on that cheek and he turned to catch her mouth, not letting this chance escape him. His arms wound their way about her and pulled her onto his lap; somehow they finally found themselves in sync. Their first proper kiss was more mature than she had expected—it started as an offer, a give hoping for a take that built up into a desperate assault on each other. When they finally stopped, both were short of breath but unwilling to pull apart; Sarah's hands were tangled in Seichi's hair and his were firmly gripping her waist, bringing their bodies against each other in such a way that Sarah couldn't help but notice the heat radiating from the rather impressive erection pressing insistently against her through her dress.

"Walking back to you is the hardest thing that I can do..." The CD that had been playing quietly in the background suddenly changed to a very familiar track by The Jesus and Mary Chain, making the pair laugh.

"Do you want me to be your plastic toy?" Seichi asked, a smile creasing the corners of his eyes. "I'm a bit older now, not quite in my prime, though."

"I don't mind a few gray hairs, Seichi, you're still a handsome devil."

He smiled hopefully and shrugged out of his leather jacket, then as Sarah stood, stripped off his long-sleeve shirt, releasing the scent of his cologne into the air until Sarah felt surrounded by the familiar, very alluring scent of this man.

"I never did show you my tattoos, did I?" he asked, the faded ink on both pecs demonstrating his first rebellion against Japanese cultural norms in his youth. The dragon and phoenix, both such proud creatures, reminded Sarah why she had fallen for Seichi all those years ago and she smiled.

"I always wondered about that, Seichi."

"Well, I had a feeling of what would happen if I was ever shirtless around you," he said, his voice taking on that lusty tone that it had in the bookstore. "And it was safer to keep you at a distance because I didn't know what I wanted then."

Sarah laughed as she too dropped her jacket and pulled her dress off over her head, revealing a black lace bra and skull-print boy shorts—a set that she had worn for comfort rather than sex appeal. She tossed the dress aside and turned around to show off all the ink she had added over the years, a body nearly fully decorated in scenes from Japanese mythology, kanji characters and flowers. "But you know now what you want, do you?"

"Oh god, yes..."

Seichi reached out and ran his fingers over the different patterns, over her skin, then over the thin cups of her bra, his touch hardening her nipples as his mouth covered hers once more. They quickly found themselves kissing like teenagers—passionate yet fumbling. Her bra joined the pile on the floor as she roughly tugged Seichi's belt open, her hands pulling the heavy material down over his hips, releasing his cock from its black cotton prison. Drops of clear fluid glistened and dripped down the thick shaft she'd often wondered about and now ran her hand over, feeling the twitching and throb of his pulse through the hot, hard flesh.

Seichi was far too distracted by her breasts to notice at first; he was rubbing his face against them, moaning against the supple flesh as Sarah held him to her, her free arm running over his back, feeling the taut muscles rippling under her fingertips.

Her boy shorts were soaked, her nerves burning in anticipation of more of his touch. When his hand found its way between her legs, Sarah gasped at the jolt of pleasure that ricocheted through her. Seichi moved his thick fingers slowly, exploring her before pulling off her shorts, leaving her fully exposed in the middle of the shop. Precome dripped down her hand as she tugged at his erection, while his thick fingers moved slowly and purposefully over her clit. He started to thrust against her hand; he was moaning and began to slip his fingers inside Sarah's dripping slit. She sighed—his fingers were stroking her in all the right places.

"Sarah...ah, you're so wet..." Seichi panted, "I want you so much...I...oh god." He thrust harder into her hand and Sarah let go, stepping back from his fingers. She couldn't believe this was happening—what an absurdly normal day it had started out as, and now, well, she hadn't expected any of this to ever be possible.

"I want you too, now, Seichi. I don't want to wait any longer." Sarah sat on the coffee table and reached out for his cock, but he pushed her hands away, a self-assured smile on his lips.

"If this is my only chance, I've got to make it my best, don't I?" he asked, as he sank to his knees on the plush black carpet.

Strong calloused hands reached out and spread her legs; he pulled her forward, burying his face between her thighs. He slid his mouth over her, lapping at the soft folds as he held her firmly in place. His tongue traced over her most sensitive spots—he quickly found them and sent Sarah's whole body tingling. She was undone, she couldn't escape from his touch and as his intensity built she couldn't hold back and came; her legs trembled and her hips quaked as he refused to stop. A second wave overtook her and she came again, her juices dripping down over her thighs and into his mouth.

By the time he released her, Sarah was panting and glistening with sweat; she'd lost count of how many times she had come, and was desperate to have more of him. "Seichi, where did you learn to do that?" she managed, her voice hoarse from moaning.

Seichi stood and looked her in the eyes as he licked his lips, that smile back to tease her. "I always wondered what you would taste like," he whispered as he climbed over her onto the table, straddling her waist. "Like that time we went driving in the mountains. I wanted to taste you out in the fresh air, with no one else around for miles." He reached down and pushed her breasts together, massaging them between his hands. "The time never seemed right for it, but now we have time, don't we?"

"Yes, mmm, Seichi, ah…please," was all Sarah could say as he began rolling her nipple with one hand, the other gripping his erection firmly, stroking himself over her. Sarah reached up and pressed her breasts together, her pink nipples darkened and taut from his touch.

"Good girl, keep them like that for me," he instructed as he lowered himself and thrust his cock between them.

The combined sensation of his hardness and the heat—it was almost unbearable. She tipped her chin downward watching him pump his hips forward and darted her tongue out, hoping to catch a taste of him. He was seeping so much precome that her chest was slick with it, the natural lubricant allowing him to push freely. Seichi gripped her breasts, his hands moving over and around hers. When she looked up at him, his head was thrown back, eyes closed, and he seemed lost in the action.

She was certain he would come on her breasts, or at least let her drink him down, but he stopped abruptly. Relinquishing his grip and rising to his feet, his cock throbbed, and drops fell onto her as he bent down and kissed her roughly, his lips bruising hers with the force. They were entangled, their bodies pressed together so tightly that it was hard to say where one stopped and the other began. The kisses went on and on; Sarah felt a desperate need to keep him close, and she could feel the same coming from him, too. Whatever happened next, this day was already the start of something big.

Far too soon, he stood up and pulled her to her feet, holding her as his hands ran down her body appreciatively. He cupped her butt, squeezing it and pressing his cock between her thighs, moving slowly against her. They turned around; it was as though they were dancing until he sat down on the edge of the coffee table. He reached up and stroked his hands over her hips, guiding her forward until Sarah hovered over his twitching cock—god, how she'd longed for that ever since they'd met.

That first joining was unbelievable; Sarah was filled with him and she sighed contentedly as he moaned a low rumble that echoed in her ear. They embraced each other for a moment, and then he whispered, "Now, bounce yourself on my cock, Sarah."

She did as he asked; the ability to be in control at a time like this was getting her off. He held her waist firmly, his face rubbing against her breasts and neck, the stubble on his chin rough but ticklish on the sensitive skin. She rode him as hard and deep as she could until her muscles were quivering and she had to stop or risk falling off.

"Tired?" he asked when she couldn't move anymore.

She nodded and Seichi helped her to stand, then joined her. They kissed again and somehow slid down each other's bodies until they were lying on the floor together, the thin fibers of the carpet feeling cool and soft on her bare flesh. He ran his hand down over her side and raised her leg, then slid himself inside her once again. Sarah moaned and sank into the feeling as he kissed along her neck and his hands went all over her body, possessing her fully.

The force of his thrusts caused Sarah to shudder and her hand went to her clit, stroking herself until she began to come around him. It was incredible, better than anything that she had imagined. His expression said he was fighting against the clenching and tightening, struggling to go deeper and maintain his control. He pushed, grinding inside her as he growled, then bit her shoulder, leaving a passionate bite mark as he came, emptying himself. He kept thrusting, as though his body were on autopilot, moving until he was certain that they were both satiated.

Lying on the rug still connected, they barely spoke. Their hands lazily trailed over each other's bodies and it was only when goose bumps began to break out that they arose. Seichi was in the middle of fastening his belt while Sarah pulled her panties on.

"Sarah, I shouldn't have...I hope I didn't rush this. I don't want to ruin it." Seichi looked shocked, a mild wave of postcoital panic washing over his features.

She smiled. "It's fine, Seichi," she said, and shrugged as she straightened out the hem of her dress. "Second chances don't come along every day. Whatever comes of this, I'm ready for it."

PHOTOGRAPHS

Jillian Boyd

There were only so many longing looks she could take from him. Rachel gathered her equipment and excused herself to the groom-to-be and his groomsmen, mumbling something about having to change the film in her camera—even though it was entirely digital. As she dashed down the corridors of the hotel back to her room, she mentally cursed herself. That was the fourth time she had used that ridiculous excuse today. Frankly she was amazed they hadn't cottoned on to it yet.

She fumbled with the key card, having to swipe it three times before the light came on and the lock clicked open. Carefully putting away her equipment, she not-so-carefully threw herself down on the bed, grunting at making an impact on the hard mattress.

"Why?" she groaned into the room. "Of all the people in the world, why him?"

It wasn't the first time she had done that. She knew it wouldn't be the last time either.

She'd suspected something from the moment she'd heard the

groom-to-be's last name. It sounded awfully similar to a name she thought was buried far away in her past. The name of a man whose lips she could still taste when she thought about them hard enough. The name of a man who had whispered his undying love to every single inch of her naked body, many times over.

She had brushed it away as a silly coincidence. It wasn't *him* that was getting married.

It turned out she was right. It was his brother.

She'd been dreading the weekend of the wedding ever since. And it wasn't like she could just nip off at any moment's notice. She was the wedding photographer—and she had agreed to be there at every single point, documenting the entire joyous occasion for the bride, groom and attending families.

Including his brother, who was serving as best man.

She had hoped that maybe, somehow, Benedict wouldn't recognize her. That the intervening seven years would have erased her from his memory. It was stupid to hope that, of course. From the moment the bride enthusiastically introduced her to the family, squeaking, "This is Rachel! She's so brilliant!" in her harsh German accent, she knew she was done for. The rest of the family had no clue as to who she was, apart from just the photographer. Benedict, however...

"Rachel?"

His face lit up as soon as he laid eyes on her. "God, Rachel, I can't believe..."

"Hello!" she said, shaking his hand with the fervor of a *luchador* shaking up his opponent. "I'm Rachel Hahn, the photographer!"

"Rachel, I know who you are..."

"Are you the brother of the bride then? How lovely! You look like the perfect best man," she continued, not giving him the chance to speak. Benedict looked utterly puzzled as Rachel excused herself for the first of many times and went off to her room.

But of course he followed her. Of course he stopped her at the elevators. Of course he smelled of that exact same silky crisp perfume as he had, way back when.

"Seven years and you won't even acknowledge me? Rachel, I thought with what we had..."

"Please don't do this to me. Just pretend..."

"I don't know you? You're not here? We're not who we were? We didn't make love on the dewy park grass while the sun came up in Vienna?"

"Vienna was a long fucking time ago, Benedict. And so was Paris. And Rome and...wherever else we went that summer. Just...don't."

She stepped into the elevator, watching the door close on the most beautiful man in the world, his face weighted by sadness. She made it all the way into the shower before she let herself break down and cry.

That was Thursday. The wedding was Saturday afternoon. Rachel sighed again, as she curled up on her bed.

"Why didn't I just...fuck it."

She closed her eyes, blocking out the world but letting in the exact memories she was trying to avoid.

"Bendy!"

Benedict pinched the bridge of his nose, trying to stave off a headache. It was entirely too hot outside. Combine that with the fact that the love of his life, a woman who he thought he had lost forever, had been hired as the photographer for his brother's wedding, and Ben was surprised he hadn't yet keeled over with a banging migraine.

"What is it, George?" he groaned, lifting himself off the sofa in their suite. His brother stood, grinning, wearing his poshest cricket outfit. He knew what was coming.

"You up for a game?"

"Let's see. It's about nine hundred degrees outside...I'm not feeling well...and, oh yes, I absolutely hate cricket. So, no."

"Ah, come on. It's a bit of fun. Anna really wants to learn."

"I don't believe for one minute Anna wants to learn how to play cricket." said Ben, lying down on the bed and wincing at the impact against the hard mattress.

"She really does! Come on, it'll be a laugh. We'll get Dad to teach her. And we're having Rachel take pictures of it all."

Ben winced again. "Then I *definitely* don't want to come."

"Why not? I've seen you looking at her, all wistful and longing. She's lovely, you're...acceptable. Go for it!"

"George, I'm not going to hook up with your wedding photographer."

"I'm just trying to help, Bendy. I can't remember the last time I've seen you happy about...well, anything, really."

"Would that be about seven years ago?"

"I'm not keeping track of your mood swings, brother dear," said George, sticking his tongue out like a little kid. George was thirty-two years old. Surprisingly. "I'm going to teach my wife-to-be how to wield a cricket bat. If you want to grace us with your presence, we're on the south court."

"Right. Do I bring ice packs and arnica cream, just in case Anna gets a little too enthusiastic with her swing?"

George rolled his eyes and left for the courts. Benedict sighed, gazing at the ceiling. Rachel Hahn. Seven years ago, Rachel Hahn walked into his life and flipped it completely upside down. She was the love of his life. And he'd been the idiot who walked away from the one thing he had been sure about.

So it was a kind of kismet that both of them ended up here, at the same time, with Rachel being the photographer for his brother's wedding to Anna. He wondered if it was a second chance, handed to him on a silver platter.

And he cursed his brother for the umpteenth time. Not that George knew about Benedict's history with Rachel. For a brief second, he debated telling his brother and going home, where his heart would lie broken but safe.

But that would have been taking the easy, cowardly way out. Again.

Despite having set herself up in a shadier corner of the south court, Rachel felt like an egg slowly frying underneath the late afternoon heat. She wasn't sure why George insisted she take candid pictures of a family cricket game—especially since she was only here to shoot the wedding and the preparations. This was not in her plans.

Nevertheless, it was their weekend, so Rachel had obliged. And from the looks of it, Benedict wasn't anywhere to be seen. After all that tension, it was a definite plus. As she watched George trying to help Anna get to grips with the bat, she took in a deep breath. The sweet scent of summer blossoms hung heavily in the air, and the heat draped over her shoulders like a comfortable duvet in winter.

She liked it here, where the shade protected her just enough. If she could, she would fall asleep in this spot, although taking a nap on the job wouldn't exactly be professional. But her eyes felt leaden and her lips dry. Maybe just a little nap? Or a drink, at least?

"Rachel! Can you come and set up here? I want some close-ups of the field," yelled Anna. Rachel squinted.

"I can take close-ups from here, you know, Anna. Since I've got a zoom lens and all."

"Yes, but really up close! I want...how do you say...*eine sehr gute Sicht auf unser Glück*."

Rachel wasn't entirely sure that *a very good view of our happiness* was something you'd see on pictures of a cricket game that so far had featured more cursing and falling over than an afternoon spent ice-skating. But she gamely pottered around and adjusted her setup to suit Anna's wishes.

As the game continued, accompanied by more falling and cursing, Rachel found herself wishing for sun cream—the sun began to feel less like a comfortable duvet in winter and more like the reflection of a large magnifying glass intent upon melting her. She hadn't counted on this kind of heat at all.

Just as she hadn't counted on Benedict's sudden appearance.

He ambled down the steps leading toward the court, giving a courteous nod toward his brother and Anna. Then he locked eyes with her, seemingly hell-bent on talking, which was exactly what Rachel had been trying to avoid. A tense knot formed in her chest, not helped by the relentless sun seemingly turning the south court into a tropical beach resort.

"Rachel. I was... Are you all right?"

She was not all right. Her legs wobbled like jelly, head spinning and mouth dry. She felt herself falling and blacking out, but somehow the collision never registered. There were only two strong, safe arms, breaking her fall.

"Rach..."

She must have been dreaming. She must have actually fallen asleep in the warm grass on the south court. She could hear a deep, languid voice calling her name, followed by a *tap tap tap* which was almost musical.

"Going...water."

Water? Oh yes, that what she needed. If she could only lift her head and sit up... Wait. Why did everything feel so heavy? And where was she?

She blinked, slowly coming back to herself. Same hard

mattress...same duvet covers...still in Sanderson Lodge, still had a wedding to photograph. So that must have meant...

"You've woken up! Christ, I was worried about you."

Oh, for fuck's sake, she thought. It had to be him catching her, and it had to be him bringing her to his room. Benedict's green eyes were full of concern, his hand brushing over her forehead. "Blimey, you've caught the sun on your face. And here I thought you were never without Factor 50."

"I wasn't expecting to use Factor 50 at a British countryside wedding," she grumbled, slowly sitting up. "God, I could murder a drink right now."

Without missing a beat, Benedict handed her a glass of water. "If you want something stronger, I could always break into the mini-fridge. It would cost me five pounds a bottle, but I'll do anything you want just to make you stay and talk to me."

He looked like a particularly hopeful puppy, gazing into her eyes with the words *Please talk to me* written in his glance. Rachel took a huge gulp of water, having every intention of standing up and walking back out, but something kept her rooted to the hard mattress. Something that she hadn't felt in forever and was damn sure not expecting to feel right now.

A slight sympathy toward Benedict had won her over. "All right. Talk. Tell me why you didn't show up. Tell me why you left me alone in a station in Zagreb. Tell me why you chose exactly that particular day to break my heart, because I've been trying to figure that out for the last seven years and, wouldn't you know it, I haven't a fucking clue."

Benedict took a deep breath and then said the exact words she'd not been waiting to hear from him for the last seven years. "I don't know, Rachel. I guess I was scared."

"Right. I'm going now." she replied, this time managing to stand up. "Have a lovely time and a lovely life."

"I was twenty-one, Rachel! I had no fucking clue what I was doing with my life! And then you came in, and suddenly everything seemed to fall into place, and that bloody scared the shit out of me!"

"Don't you think I was scared too? Because, believe me, I was absolutely terrified to death! I felt something in my heart that I haven't felt ever since, and you just walked away from it!"

"Because I was a stupid bastard! And I still am, because I'm fully expecting you to do the same and walk out of my life again and I can't take losing you twice!"

"Well, then you're wrong because I am staying right here!"

"Good!"

"Good!"

"I'm going to kiss you now!"

"Jesus Christ, it's about time!"

Benedict strode forward and pulled Rachel toward him. In the split second before their lips met, she could swear he whispered a thank-you to the divine graces, as their kiss seemingly melted the seven intervening years to a puddle of nothing.

His hands roamed over her body, as if remapping her curves into his head. He hadn't changed; his touches were deliberate and careful enough, but still hungry and wanting. Rachel moaned into his mouth, shivers of deep lust running down the back of her spine. She wanted him to take her right then and there, to throw her on the bed and ravish her as befitted a posh country hotel like this.

Already she could feel his cock hard against her, straining at his fly and begging to be let out. God, his cock. She kicked herself for temporarily forgetting just how glorious it was. She wanted to reach out for it, release it and take it in her mouth like the last time was only yesterday.

But then she pulled herself away. Her breathing was heavy,

her panties were soaked with her juices, her clit was crying out for his fingers...and here she was, having second thoughts.

"Rachel?"

Surprising herself, she uttered, "I'm so sorry...I don't think I can."

Her feet took control, and she was out of the room before Benedict even had time to think about what had just happened. It was only when she found her way back into her own room that her heart took over and the tears flowed freely.

"Bendy! Practicing your best man speech, I see?"

Benedict didn't look up from his piece of paper. The only way he acknowledged that his brother had joined him was a little wave in his direction.

He wasn't practicing his speech. He was reading it, possibly for the thirteenth time that week, but he wasn't practicing it. He wasn't even sure if the words on the paper were actual words.

George sat down next to him at the table in the hotel bar and put a brotherly hand on his shoulder. Benedict could tell that he'd switched gears from "teasing asshole" to "loving brother" mode.

"Are you all right, mate? You've been miles away all weekend."

"I'm right here, George."

"You know what I mean, Ben. Come on, I'm your brother. I can literally *feel* whenever you're having an existential moment. You get all frowny and maudlin. Like right now."

He felt ashamed to admit that George had it spot on. Benedict could actually feel the intensity of his own frown. He pinched the bridge of his nose.

"Sorry, George. I didn't mean to be like this on your big weekend. It's just..."

George looked at him expectantly. He considered just letting it all out and telling him everything there was to tell about Rachel and their shared history...and the future he had virtually kissed goodbye.

"It's just a bit busy for me. Never mind me; I'm just an old hermit."

"You're a twenty-eight-year-old journalist. Neither old nor a hermit, Bendy. If you want to talk, I'm right here. It may be my wedding, but you are my brother, and I always have time for you. Remember that."

"Duly noted. Thank you."

George smiled at his brother, and then stood up again. "Now, get something fancy on. We're going on the piss and having a boys' night out. It's my last night as a bachelor and I would very much like to go out in style."

Benedict hesitated, looking from his speech to the door of the restaurant, half expecting Rachel to walk through the door and into his arms. At this point, he could only hope she was still here. She hadn't been seen all day.

"All right," he said finally. "But if I have to peel Steven up from the floor of a strip club at three in the morning again, you are in my debt, brother of mine."

"Sorted. Let's go and celebrate."

Benedict took a deep breath and followed his brother. Maybe George was right, and this would do him good. One more day and George would be married and Benedict would be on his way to his next assignment. How bad could a night of letting loose be?

It was three in the morning when Rachel heard the noise outside her hotel room window. She had fallen asleep watching some reality show on TV, after keeping to herself in her room all day. At first she thought it was the television, but then why would the man flogging vacuum cleaners on the home shopping channel scream out her name?

"Rachel!"

"What the hell?"

Rachel scrambled out of bed, rubbing her eyes. There it was again.

"Rachel!"

Followed by loud sobbing. As Rachel tried to focus her eyes, she made out three shapes sitting on a bench outside. She peeked through the open window and heard the distinct voices of Benedict and George, along with one of the other groomsmen.

"Oh god, I miss her, George!"

"It's okay, Bendy. It's okay. Just keep the noise down."

"But I'm sad!"

"I know you're sad, mate…"

"Oh god, I have missed her so much and now she doesn't want me! Don't leave me, Rachel! I love you!"

Rachel gasped.

"It's okay, brother of mine. We'll get you inside and you get some rest, okay?"

"George! I don't…"

She couldn't make out the rest of what he was saying, but what she could see spoke volumes. George and his groomsman each held on to a shoulder as they walked a still sobbing Benedict back to his room.

Rachel slowly backed away from the window and retreated to bed, wondering just how stubborn she could still afford to be.

Both of them spent the next morning playing a game of trying to catch each other's eyes without really trying. Over breakfast, from which most of the wedding party appeared to be missing, it came down to Benedict and Rachel in a standoff of longing stares and sudden glances over plates of eggs Florentine.

Rachel, who sat alone in one corner, kept her eyes on Benedict, who was in the other corner. There were times where she'd nearly worked up the courage to go up to him, but faltered. She suspected it was much the same on his end.

"Come on, Hahn," she said to herself. "You're not twenty-one and extremely awkward anymore."

No. She was twenty-eight and extremely stubborn. All she had to do was stand up and go to him. But as she readied herself, George suddenly materialized and sat himself down on the seat opposite hers. She could see Benedict doing that thing where he pinched the bridge of his nose, either in mortification or fighting off a catastrophic headache. Or both.

"Okay, I have about two minutes before I have to start preparing, so I'll make this quick. D'you mind?" said George, before stealing a slice of toast from her plate. Rachel wanted to protest, but he held his hand up and apologized before continuing.

"Ben's my younger brother. I love him to death, but he can be a stubborn and indecisive fucker sometimes. I mean, this is the bloke who once spent an hour deciding between mayonnaise and ketchup on his curly fries and then wouldn't give the mayonnaise back to me. Granted, he was nine at the time, but still."

George paused, practically devouring the toast. Rachel handed him another piece, which he gratefully accepted.

"But here's the thing. In all my life, in all the years I've had Ben as my brother, I have never seen him so sure about anything than about what he feels for you."

"He was drunk, George. I heard you guys outside."

"Of course you did. I think the entire hotel heard him, he was that loud. But he was telling the truth, Rachel. Trust me on that. I know my brother well enough to know when his heart's been properly stolen by someone. Which reminds me, I have to go and get dressed to marry the woman who's stolen mine. See you in a tick."

Before George left, he shot them both a wink. Now it was Rachel pinching the bridge of her nose. What was she going to do?

**

At five to two that afternoon, Rachel had set up on the lawn of the south court, where the ceremony was taking place. The heat outside was mercifully less scorching, but the heat inside her body was agonizing. The guests were already streaming in, with Anna's parents proudly welcoming what looked like the entire population of a small German village to the proceedings.

The bride herself looked amazing. The groom, currently waiting at the front, looked incredibly dapper in his suit. And Benedict...he was the reason she was burning. It wasn't just the suit and tie, or the slicked-back hair, or any one specific detail. It was him. It was the way he looked at her as he walked past her. It was the way he was handling George's sudden onset of nerves. It was the way he just...was.

It made her realize how much she'd missed him...and how much more she would miss him if she let him slip away.

But she didn't have time to think about that now. For the next few hours, she would be an exemplary professional.

And then she'd get her man. At last.

"Rachel, thank you so much. You have such...*ein gutes Auge für einen schönen Moment.* Thank you."

Anna pulled Rachel into a hug that was surprisingly strong for such a slight lady. For a moment she feared bruising.

"Thank you for having me. Have a lovely time in... Where is it you're going?"

"Vienna. Benedict's recommendation. Apparently he had the most beautiful night of his life there."

"Right," Rachel said, nodding, but feeling her heart sink into the ground. She hadn't seen Benedict since the dinner ended; the fear that he might have left without her noticing weighed on her shoulders.

"Anna, I don't suppose you've..."

But before Rachel could finish, someone called out for the bride. Anna apologized and dashed off toward the party marquee. Rachel sighed, took her equipment and made her way back toward the hotel. She never tended to overstay her welcome, and as far as this wedding was concerned, her job was done.

She was leaving the next day. And it looked a lot like she'd be leaving brokenhearted.

But as she walked up the steps, that heart started to race. Coming down the steps was Benedict, carrying his bags. Upon seeing her, he shook his head and started walking faster.

"Hey! Hey, where the hell do you think you're going!" she shouted, chasing him to the little copse nearby.

"Home."

"No!"

Rachel grabbed on to his arm but Benedict shook himself free. "Please don't make this harder for me than it already is, Rachel."

"What, you leaving me again? Walking out of my life for the second time? No, no, you are not going to do that!"

"You don't want me, Rachel!"

"Yes, I do!"

Both of them stopped in their tracks, on the other side of the green.

"Yes," Rachel repeated. "I do want you. I want to curse you. I want to swear at you, I want to take you by the shoulders

and shake sense into you! But most of all, I want you to throw
me down on the green and make love to me, because what I
want right now and forever is you!"

"Brilliant! Great! Shall I just throw you down and take you
right here then?"

"Dear god, yes!" she said for the second time that weekend.

There was a clattering of bags on to the grass, followed by
Benedict pulling Rachel into his arms.

"For real this time?" he asked, his eyes again filled with
hope.

Her answer was her kiss, her lips melting together with his.
The late evening air was still thick with warmth, and Rachel's
head swam as Benedict kissed her deeply. Remaining hints of
setting sun illuminated his face and his gorgeous curls, making
them almost shine.

The kiss seemed to last for ages. As they finally parted, both
of them left with ragged breaths, Benedict's arms wrapped
around her waist, pulling her close enough so she could feel
the outline of his growing erection against her mound. He took
off his suit jacket and spread it out on the ground. He fumbled
with the buttons of his shirt and eventually managed to bare
his gorgeous chest, flecked with dark hairs and still so beautifully defined.

Rachel's mouth formed a perfect O, as memories of that
fateful night in Vienna flooded back. He was wearing a suit
jacket that day as well. They had gone to the ballet and ended
up in the park, under the trees, sweaty and tangled up.

"And before you ask, yes, that is the same suit jacket I wore
in Vienna. I'm just that nostalgic," he said, grinning sheepishly.

"I thought it looked familiar," said Rachel, sinking down
on the spread-out jacket. "Then again, I've fantasized about
this goddamn jacket for god-knows-how-long now."

"Was I wearing it in your fantasies?" he asked, straddling

her hips and pulling up her skirt. Already the feeling of his fingers brushing the wet fabric of her panties made her shiver with pleasure.

"No. We were fucking on it."

With one deft pull, her panties found their way onto the ground, leaving her spread open and ready for Benedict's cock. She fumbled with his belt, eventually managing to release his erection from his boxers. He briefly let his fingers dance over her cleft, relishing in how wet she was.

Then he flipped her over, guiding her onto her hands and knees. There was a brief, agonizing pause in which Rachel heard the distinctive sound of a foil wrapper being opened. And then there was the feeling of his cock, sliding inside her with ease.

Both of them breathed a sigh of relief and anticipation before Benedict started fucking her. Rachel's hand found her throbbing clit, her fingers vigorously frigging herself as his cock thrust into her. He moaned her name like a lustful mantra, as he held on to her hips to steady himself.

In the distance, there was the light and sound of revelers, celebrating a new union. Here, in the relative darkness of the copse, there were two people celebrating a reunion. The notion of getting caught was far away from Rachel's mind—this man had made love to her on the banks of the Seine, in an alleyway in Amsterdam, near the Riesenrad in the Prater Park... With Benedict, she feared nothing.

Their movements became faster and more frantic, as Rachel chased the light of her climax with every stroke of her fingers and every thrust of his cock. Benedict's grunts became almost feral as he fought off his own climax.

"I can't hold myself much longer, Rachel," he moaned. "I can't."

"It's okay. Come inside me," she gasped, just as her own

orgasm took over and rushed through her entire body. She rode it out as Benedict's thrusts became nearly brutal, before his body stiffened and his cock twitched with his own rapture. He cried out her name, into the trees and into forever. It was like he could breathe again, after spending so long under water.

"This time, for real," Rachel whispered, before collapsing onto the jacket. Benedict laughed.

"So, you're a journalist now?"

"Yeah. It almost sounds grown-up, doesn't it? Foreign correspondent, Benedict Matheson."

After their tryst on the grass, Rachel had dragged Benedict to her hotel room, where they'd spent the entire night trying to make up for seven lost years. In the morning, he could barely walk, much to her amusement. A hearty breakfast was a definite necessity in this case.

"That's incredibly fancy. It's what you've always wanted, wasn't it?"

"Well, either that or working for MI5," said Benedict, before taking another bite of toast. "Either way, I wanted to travel. What about you? Don't you ever want to strike out again? Take pictures of things other than weddings?"

"I haven't really thought of that, to be honest."

"And why not? You're incredibly talented, and the world is as beautiful as you are."

He took her hand in his. "Come with me."

"Where to?"

"My next assignment. Three weeks in Los Angeles. I fly out on Tuesday."

"Benedict...but, are you absolutely sure?"

"I have never been surer about anything in my entire life than about you, Rachel Hahn. I love you. Always have. And I want you to come with me."

"What about afterward?"

Benedict grinned. "Taking it slow, getting reacquainted, being a couple, being in love. For real, this time. Building our own adventure."

Rachel couldn't help grinning herself. "I like a bit of adventure."

Two days later, as she stepped off the plane into the glorious LA sunshine, closely followed by Benedict, she knew she was in for just that—and a whole lot more.

DANISH AFFAIR

J. Crichton

In the hot, slow days of summer he arrived at our two-story home in small-town suburbia. I remember driving home with him in the backseat and my mother riding shotgun, plying him with polite, simple questions about his journey and pointing out the local landmarks. He seemed interested though, eyes widening and face against the glass, staring out at that awful copper statue that had gone green with age and the local diner that I had passed every day of my life.

He did weird things like sleep on top of the covers and not eat his avocados at dinner. Even his underwear was foreign and fascinating to me; pulling them out of the laundry was thrilling and amusing. I held his briefs and giggled while my mother would mistake the teenage obsession I was developing for bullying and chide me for it. "Now, now. They're just different, that's all."

She saw him as a pet in some ways; an exotic blond sixteen-year-old pet known by all the locals as Andy. I called him Andy too, though sometimes I called him Anders because I liked the sound. My mouth was not used to such exotic things and soon I longed to taste more than his name.

"Tell me about your country," I asked him while we sat on my bed and watched videos on my laptop. His eyes were the same kind of blue that could be found in our boring town and yet to me they were the eyes of a Viking.

"Denmark? It's just pigs and cheese and alternative energy." And so it was to him, but it built up in my mind as this magical place of Hamlet and Lego and old gods. He told me about Shakespeare's ill-fated prince and his real, still standing, castle. My world was small and he made it big. I used to lie on my back on the guest bed—his bed then—dreaming of running away with this worldly boy by my side.

In the years that followed I would think back on the most arbitrary details about him, like how incredibly large his hands were, how good he was at backflips off of walls and how his jokes were awful but still made me laugh. I thought of how he used to play my father's guitar and sing songs about shooting stars in a language I hadn't understood at all. And then I would remember things like being out with my friends or watching movies with my boyfriend and thinking of the light on Anders's hair, and I would wonder why the guy I'd had a crush on since I was eight years old was suddenly not good enough. None of my friends got it either; to them he was just this goofy, lanky boy with a funny accent. To me he was an awakening.

There was a school dance in November about a month before he left. It was semiformal, meaning the guys wore chinos and button-up shirts and the girls wore things they would be embarrassed to admit to ten years down the road. One of my friends was crying rivers of mascara after being rejected. No fewer than seven of her peers were in attendance on the stairs, decrying the evils of men while glancing hopefully through the glass doors leading back to the dance floor. I had enough love issues of my own and I had misplaced Eric, my so-called boyfriend.

Alone, I returned to the hired DJ and disco lights. I watched from afar while familiar faces clung to each other and slow-danced, or else sucked face until a chaperone pulled them apart. Anders came over amid all this with a half-finished orange soda in one hand and my father's best dress shirt on. The effect was decidedly uncool, but it made my blood race nonetheless. "Do you want to dance?"

The soda can went in the corner and I followed my Danish exchange student out onto the floor where his skin glowed first pink then orange, blue then yellow under the changing lights. Around my waist his hands were sweaty and being that close I first realized how perfectly my head fit into the crook of his shoulder. His body was hot, as though he were running a fever, but I didn't mind a bit as he held me tight and set his chin upon the top of my head.

I felt something insistent pressing against my hip—once it dawned on me what it was, the shape was unmistakable. I mean, if I'd pulled away at that time everyone would have noticed it in profile, it was that obvious. Those chinos weren't hiding anything. He didn't say anything about it and so neither did I, even though my emotions were shifting like strobe lights between panic and thrill.

The song drew slowly to an end as we rotated in an equally lazy circle. I felt him lean down and whisper in my ear, "Could you give me a moment before you pull away?"

Of course I agreed, taking the time to bask in the scent of his cologne and trying not to cry at the thought that Anders was leaving in a month. We were back to being wallflowers by the time my boyfriend arrived; he had been hanging around in the art hallway doing things that weren't half as cool as he and his friends thought they were.

My date took one look between Anders and me and handed me a grape soda, which seemed at that moment too sweet and too cloying—too much. I stared at the floor and avoided Eric's hand when he reached for it, all the while terrified that he'd notice that Anders's fingers kept brushing against the ones on my left.

"Hey man, I just want to talk to her for a moment, is that okay?" Andy asked. He was gesturing toward the stairs just recently vacated.

"Why can't you say whatever you want to say in front of me?" Eric's hand curled possessively around mine while Anders took the other and suddenly I realized that my secret desperation for the boy who slept down the hall from me hadn't been so secret after all. And I, young, foolish and unprepared for consequences, started to cry. All I could think of was that one or all of us would be hurt by my actions.

"Look," insisted Anders, "She's crying now. I'm going to go talk to her." He'd rolled up his shirtsleeves sometime earlier and the dance-floor lights glinted off of the faint gold hair on his arms. I felt another pang of desire because Anders was there to take me away from it all again.

The staircase was cold and lit with harsh fluorescents, but we hid under it in a dusty corner and shivered, each daring the other to be the first to speak.

"You could come stay with me in Denmark if you want," he said in a voice full of shaky hope. "You could do a home-stay next and I could teach you Danish for real. And you could be um—"

I remember the way his face crinkled as he said it, as though it were physically painful to say something so mortifying. "You could be my girl, if you want."

"But I'm going to university here," I said, mostly afraid of what my mother would say if she knew I had run off with the exchange student. She could tell at this point how madly in love with him I was and did not approve.

"I care about you," he tried again.

"I care about you, too," I said. He was holding both of my hands by then and they felt so huge, so warm and calloused. He was everything I wanted.

"But I think I'm in love with you," he blurted.

"I love you too," I said sadly. He reached up and stroked my cheek as I'd fallen to pieces again, a sobbing drama queen of her own making.

Eric pushed his way into the alcove with a single disapproving glare and that was that. My dad came to pick Andy and me up from the dance and we were silent the whole way home. To him it might just have been youth but his words stayed with me all the years that came afterward, through all the people that came and went in my life. On my path to adulthood I would think back on Anders and the day he left.

On his bedside table he had placed a letter to my parents on some sort of fancy yellow paper I guess he'd brought with him, thanking them for their hospitality and saying that he would never forget us. The sheets on his bed were made perfectly and he had tidied away any signs of his presence save an unopened packet of tissues from when he'd caught a cold earlier in the month. I'd gone into his room to give him his Christmas present but I was devastated at what I saw, at the hole he was about to leave in my life.

No more mysterious foreign phrases or silly faces, no more backflips or serenades with Dad's guitar. No more good ol' Andy. It hurt me far worse than the dance; the idea that I would lose his everyday presence from my life. Anders came in to say goodbye and found me red-faced and sniffling on his bedspread. He sat down next to me and pulled me into a hug. "Don't cry," he said gently, as though addressing a small child.

"It'll be okay. You'll be okay without me."

I said nothing and handed him his present. "Open it when you get back to Copenhagen." I didn't want to see gratitude feigned or real on his face because it would be too final.

"Here's yours then, but I didn't wrap it." From his pocket he produced the treasured necklace he always wore around his neck, with the pendant in the shape of Thor's hammer. He set it around my neck and kissed my forehead as the airbus outside gave a honk. "You've got my number. We'll keep in touch, *Frøken Stjernestøv.*"

Andy called me once on a Saturday morning, saying he couldn't talk long because his parents were worried about the bill. He said that things were back to normal over there but he missed me and missed the school. He asked me to call him next time, and I was walking on roses until I realized I couldn't find his contact information anywhere.

I searched the entire house; days passed and I turned our home upside down. Months passed and I began to despair, throwing myself into learning about Denmark as a country instead. The Internet then wasn't exactly the information gold-mine that it is today but I devoured all the knowledge I could find—all because I couldn't find Anders.

University came and went and with it new boyfriends and new perspectives, but I never forgot about that boy. I graduated and moved to Denmark, got a job and a life and settled there. I learned the language, slept with plenty of Danish men and even after exotic became standard I still wanted him. Fifteen full years passed of periodically typing *Anders Christensen* into search engines until suddenly—finally—he appeared on a website dedicated to photography.

His hometown and birthday matched! It was him! I hyper-ventilated for a few minutes, clicked the contact button and sent off the least stalkerish message I could think of:

*Remember me? You lived at my house for six months
in high school. I accidentally lost your contact info
and I wondered how you've been all these years.
Great photography! Anyway, I live in Denmark
now, how about you?*

As if all of my incredible awkwardness at the thought of him
wasn't a subtext to that entire message.

A few hours later I got a cheerful note about how it was good
to hear from me and how we should catch up. Shamelessly, I
texted his number right away.

*Whoa! How times have changed! I remember the dance and
your boyfriend was so angry, haha. Oh, and chemistry class—
my sleeve caught fire once.* Two seemingly random memories,
but he'd mentioned "the incident" and there had to be something to that, so I swallowed my cowardice and invited him out.

Sure, he wrote, twenty minutes later. *I'll pick you up after
work tomorrow?* I gave him my office address, stared at my
phone for a few minutes and tried to sleep.

Panic returned as the clock rounded seven the following
evening and I knew intuitively that he was waiting outside. The
daylight had taken the day's warmth and I pulled my coat up
around my neck to block out the chill. It had been raining and
the streetlights reflected in puddles as I exited the office and
descended the staircase. In the shadows stood a broad-shoul-
dered and faceless figure looking at the ground, and I had a split
second of doubt. Was dredging up old memories the best thing
to do after all this time?

And then he looked up and beneath that side-swept blond
fluff was Anders, with the same mischievous blue eyes and
crooked smile. To me no time had passed, though the night hid
gentle crinkles and a five o'clock shadow that might've been on
purpose.

"Hey," I said. He pulled me into a hug and my first thought was that his cologne was different but underneath it was the scent of the Andy I knew, resurrected from my past. I felt alive—and just as nervous and wonderful as the first time.

Then I thought, as he whispered, "I miss you," in my ear, how his torso was thicker; more solid. More of a man than the Anders I had once known.

"I missed you too," I said in a daze. "Losing your address was one of the biggest regrets of my life."

He barked out a laugh. "Is that what happened? I should have guessed." A white rain-spattered road bike sat next to him and he climbed on. "Get on and I'll take you somewhere out of the wet."

"How?"

"On the back of course." He looked over his shoulder and grinned. "The luggage rack is plenty sturdy unless the thought of putting your arms around me makes you uncomfortable."

"No!" I said a little too quickly. I wished I hadn't worn a skirt and heels, but he pulled a handkerchief out of his pocket and laid it on my makeshift seat and then we were off, wobbling at first then moving through the streets of a city I was now seeing with new eyes.

"I guess I should have realized you'd lost it," he called into the wind, pedaling hard in time to turn a corner. I held Anders tighter, relishing the texture of his pea coat and the body moving underneath. "I just assumed I'd made you uncomfortable after—well."

"No! No, never." I pressed my face against his back and sighed. "Never that."

"Really?" Our urban chariot suddenly drew to a stop. I climbed off, thinking we'd arrived—but there weren't any shops and not a single soul around us. Leftover raindrops fell from the awning and Anders's breath was a fine mist in the chilly air. "I really thought I'd misread everything with you. If I hadn't been so stubborn—"

"If I hadn't been so forgetful—"

"Then I might not have wasted fifteen years of my life. I should have known." He squatted down, head in his hands.

"It wasn't a waste," I insisted, wondering if he was saying what I thought he was. "I've learned a lot in that time. I'm sure you have too."

He stood again and walked toward me with a gentle smile on his face. His hands closed over mine, just as huge and sinewy as they'd always been. "I have, it's true, but seeing you again it's all the same—you're still that girl. Still the same girl who held my teenage heart in her hands."

"We aren't teens anymore." His eyes were full of the fascination he had once held and of the puppy love of warm summer days on a cold autumn night. I grabbed his coat lapels and kissed him fully on the mouth, marveling as his arms wrapped around my waist and he kissed me back. His lips were dry and cool in delicious contrast to the hot, wet tongue that made its way into my mouth.

Only when it became necessary to breathe did he pull away and press his forehead to mine. "If losing my address was one of your biggest regrets, not kissing you that night was one of mine." We kissed again and I felt him smile against my mouth. "Shall I take you to that bar, now?"

I climbed onto the back of the bicycle, and when he was seated in front of me I ruffled his soft, thick hair. "No, I want to catch up on what we've missed."

He guided us through the city lights and half-frozen bystanders until he stopped at a tall, narrow building three floors high. He hurried up the staircases and I trailed behind, followed closely by my suspended disbelief. I had always wanted to see Anders's room and now with the turn of a key I was in his apartment.

"It's really small," he warned. "It's just big enough for me." He was right, too; a single dish sat by the sink and a little TV in the living-slash-bedroom, his computer in the corner and an acoustic guitar. There were posters of movies I would never have guessed he'd like and along with the photography equipment, they helped me to form an image of Anders the man, not the boy. Still, there was something about the scene that told me he hadn't changed much in fifteen years.

"Would you like something to drink?" he asked, suddenly the shy host. I took off my coat and sat down on his futon.

"Um, a beer I guess?" The stereo system came on and a moment later Anders reappeared with a bottle and a remote control.

"Hang on," he said, as I took my first sip. The songs shifted through and finally settled on one I recognized but couldn't place at first.

"Is this—?" I asked with my heart in my throat. He stole my beer and took a swig, setting it aside to pull me to my feet. "Frøken Stjernestøv," he mumbled. We were dancing in a slow circle, kissing while he pulled my shirt over my head.

"I have no idea what that means," I said, running my hand down his chest to cup him between the legs. I wasn't entirely the shy girl he remembered, either. "Miss...?"

"Stardust." His tongue traced a slow arc just below my ear. "Miss Stardust." I moved his hands to my breasts and his lips to my mouth. I held his face in my hands and traced the muscles of his jaw that had grown sharp in adulthood, the long, straight bridge of his nose. His hips drove insistently against my thigh as he bent to hold me, groaning with hunger.

I was like a starving woman too, yanking at his belt buckle and the buttons on his shirt. My tongue was on his collarbone as he hiked up my skirt; I bit at his nipples when his fingers slipped into my panties and stroked my slit.

"Lie down," I told him, yanking down his chinos—and then I laughed aloud in sheer surprise. "You still have these?"

"Of course I do. My girlfriend in college hated these boxers— quite rightly, since they were my Christmas present from you." His eyes smoldered and suddenly the boxers were gone. I was left with a new sense of disbelief.

"So what they say about big hands is true," I said, climbing over his erection so that it could press against my underwear. It pulsed and throbbed with a life of its own, quite in time with the music playing in the corner.

"It's yours," he sighed, pulling down the cups of my bra so he could flick my nipples. "I've always wanted to see these— every time you walked by my room in a towel or in a tank top. I think I jerked off—oh god, move your hips like that again— more in that room than anywhere in my life."

"I would have liked to have seen that," I breathed, rocking back and forth over him. Arms snaked up my back and pulled me down so that he could tongue my areolas; that crooked grin never left his face.

"I can't believe this is happening," Anders murmured, breathing in the scent between my breasts. "You still drive me mad. I wish we'd done this years ago."

"Somehow I don't." I climbed off of his lap and turned my back to him, still shy as I undressed. "Teenagers always blunder through things when they're naked." I looked back at him over my shoulder, grinning as his cock jumped with interest. I wiggled my bum. "I'd much rather see what Andy can do now."

He was on his feet in an instant with a possessive growl in his throat. My left breast fell to his ministrations and his fingers stole between my legs, stroking at the wetness there and spreading it slowly while his stubbled jaw moved over my neck and shoulder. "Clench your legs," he whispered, guiding me over his fingertips. I shuddered and squirmed, sparks tingling through me in fits and starts. A finger pressed on either side of my clit to form a track as I moved my hips.

"Oh god," I gasped. "Where did you learn that?"

"Where indeed," he smiled. A drop of precome dripped onto my tailbone and I reached back, smearing it along the big mushroom head; he bucked forward in response and began to thrust against my palm. His movements were restricted though, teasing; he was giving me a taste of what he could do and nothing more. I turned to kiss him but Anders was tall and I had to crane my neck—he used the opportunity to curve his body and slide against me, thrusting his heavy cock between my thighs and buttocks.

"Think of it," he whispered feverishly as I rode his relentless digits. "We were meant to be here tonight, not a moment before. Today is the day we were meant to—oh my god, you're so wet. You're so wet."

I let out a strangled scream as my first orgasm of the night left me convulsing. "I've wanted you for so long, Anders. Even when I didn't know you anymore." Oh hell, why had that set me to tears?

"Hey," he said, turning me to face him so that I could see the earnestness in his eyes. "No more regrets, right? I'm here now. You're here now."

I turned away again and looked out over the city lights, over the world outside the window. Here was a chance, too, for tying up old ends or finding new beginnings. Anders was right.

I faced him once more and dropped to my knees, bouncing the tip of his waiting cock on the flat of my tongue, and then flicking along the head. I grabbed his thighs and looked up in time to see his eyes widen as he gasped my name. I swallowed as deeply as I could, then pulled back only to do it again and again. I bit at his thighs and stroked his hip bones until his knees began to buckle and he sank shakily onto the futon.

"Stop, stop! I'm going to—"

He reached for my shoulders and his stomach muscles clenched with the effort of holding back. But he had caught a second wind in the next breath and soon he was seated on the edge of the bed, two fingers curling inside me as I looked out once more over the city. His hands were powerful: twisting, stretching until I spread my legs farther and moved into his touch.

"Jeg vil op i dig." I want to get inside you. I readily agreed and with his hands on my hips he lowered me with an aching slowness that left no space within me for anything but him. When he was seated as deeply as he could go his kisses fell along my shoulders and he began to thrust.

"Brace yourself," he warned. I nearly laughed mid-moan, wondering what he could possibly mean, but in the next second he began to fuck me so hard my teeth clacked together. My ass bounced off of his powerful thighs and my limbs were quickly turning to jelly. He stopped for the space of a heartbeat and then started up again like a jackhammer.

It was the most delicious thing I had ever felt. Had this teenage boy I'd known turned into a machine in my absence? Filthy mumblings vibrated their way up my throat as his hands gripped my wrists, holding me steady so his hips could piston harder, faster. "Anders," I said breathlessly, "I want to look into your eyes."

"I don't know how long I'll be able to hold back if you do that." He smiled against my neck and let me up, kissing me languidly for a moment before I lay back against his pillows. I was surrounded by the same scent I had fought to keep in another bed he had once occupied.

"Is it weird to have been a little bit in love with someone for fifteen years?" I blinked at his question, and then sighed as his cock ran the length of my slit. His hands went between my legs and held me apart so that he could bump against my clit. I shivered.

"I guess not if the feelings are returned." His thrusting was rough, fast and the head of his erection was doing crazy things to my already frazzled nerves. "I used to—oh!—think I was wrong to keep holding on, though."

"The only thing left to hold on to is me," he said, finally bringing me over the edge to an orgasm so strong it left me kicking my heels against the futon. "I'm glad I was the one that got away then."

His eyes, though older, still held that mischievous twinkle of youth. My legs hooked at the ankles and he held them against his chest just as he drove into me again; all of my body could feel him—I acutely knew the shape of him now, spreading from my center through my fingers and toes.

Soon though, the muscles in his arm and back were straining and his movements had become erratic: first slow, then a series of sharp, fast thrusts, then deep as he could manage and shallow again, all to stave off a finish that I was ready to beg for under this exquisite torture. I pulled my ankles from his grasp and set them on his shoulders, reached for his hair and yanked him down, kissing him with all the urgency that I could inject.

"You're just as maddening as you always were," I whispered, arching my back as he pushed hard enough to lift my hips.

"I could never resist you," he growled back. His eyes closed briefly and he muttered something I couldn't catch.

"What?" I asked, the end of the word trailing off into a squeak as he took one nipple in his mouth and then the other.

"Jeg vil kneppe dig til din krop husker min form," he said. "I want to fuck you 'til your body remembers my shape."

I tucked my head into the crook of his neck and he held me against him, powering his way through as I was swept away in the sensation and scent, the sheen of sweat that clung to us both and the smooth expanses of muscle under my fingers.

At the last he looked up, stared directly into my eyes and froze as though stunned. A look of wonder came over his face and then was mirrored on mine as I felt him pulsating: the release had silenced him completely.

He rolled off and to the side, extending an arm in invitation. I lay with my head on his chest for a while, breathing heavily and unwilling to speak in case it broke the spell. Maybe I would wake up from this and find myself staring at the computer screen or an old photograph of a time when spaghetti strap jumpers and heavily jelled spikes were cool.

"I think," he said, reaching for the alarm clock to his left, "You and I should take tomorrow off. Obviously on a chilly night like tonight it's very easy to catch a cold."

"Oh?" I asked, amused.

"Yeah, I mean, it's been a long time and we have a lot of catching up to do. I don't remember that scar on your shoulder and you haven't seen my photography, for starters. I want to see how much Danish you've learned and see what you're like halfway down a bottle of wine now that we're old enough to drink things not from parents' liquor cabinets."

"I'd like to hear you play guitar again," I agreed. "And tell you all the drama you missed after high school."

"Sounds like fun," Anders grinned, kissing me on the forehead. "And besides, I'll need at least a full day to make sure you never forget my address again."

BEGINNINGS AND ENDINGS

Kristina Wright

It started with a text at 3:00 a.m. *I miss you.* The cynic inside me said it was a booty call text, but the realist said he'd either just come from a booty call and was feeling nostalgic or he truly missed me. Either way, I wasn't awake to get the text until the next morning. And I responded with a smile: *I miss you too. And not just at 3AM.*

We always know when a relationship begins, but sometimes the ending comes and it's not until much later that we can look back and pinpoint the end. "There," we say to ourselves. "That was the last day, that was the end." If we're lucky, we get that kind of closure. If we're lucky.

It didn't happen that way with Erik and me. There was no ending. There was the last day I saw him—in a crowded parking lot at the mall around Christmastime—and then there was... nothing. It was, at best, a tumultuous relationship. One that should never have happened, I can acknowledge in retrospect. We were in different places in our lives and we wanted different things—a fact I didn't discover until I'd already fallen in love.

He was trying to be someone he wasn't and I was trying...well, I was trying to believe he could be what I needed. It was destined to fail, but something—call it love—kept us trying. Fighting for it to work, when we weren't fighting each other.

There in that parking lot, right around Christmas, he kissed me for the last time. I was crying, as I did so often in those last few months, and he was panicked he had lost me. He kissed me and I felt...nothing. Nothing good, anyway. The passion was tamped down and muffled by so many negative emotions I couldn't even remember when his kiss—just his kiss—could make me soaking wet. That should've told me it was the end, but even then...well, we had been there before. We'd broken up three times in as many years, for weeks or even months, and somehow we always found a way back to each other. It was usually as a result of lies—to ourselves and each other—that generated false hope. But we did it anyway and for a while it worked, as make-up sex became our norm and we drowned ourselves in sensation and ignored the cold, hard truth—we just weren't meant to be together.

Until...we just didn't see each other again. We had a few phone calls that ended with one or both of us screaming, we texted each other those random *I miss you* messages, but ulti-mately they would devolve into accusations and anger. We talked about going to a concert we'd planned for before the last big blowup, but the tickets went unused—at least, I didn't go and I never had the courage to ask if he'd taken someone else—and then the texts simply tapered off to nothing. I cut him out on all social media because quitting cold turkey seemed best for both of us and having any access to his day-to-day life seemed dangerous to my mental health. I heard through the friend of a friend that he had started up with someone else, someone who he could likely be more himself with, someone who was more easy-going and less intense. At least, that's what I told myself. No way he'd find someone he loved more than me. I knew that. *Knew* it. Because I knew I'd never find anyone I loved more than him.

Time is a funny thing. They say it heals all wounds, but that's not true. I let my communication with Erik taper off to almost nothing and felt my heart scab over nicely. The first year was hell—every holiday, every place I had ever gone with him, was a bad memory. I had to remind myself, over and over, the number of times we'd spent fighting on my birthday or in a crowded restaurant. It wasn't a good relationship; I had to keep reminding myself of that. We were wrong for each other. So wrong.

Two years later and I was good. I had moved on. I had dated casually and been seeing a great guy for six months, one I liked a lot even if I didn't love him with that all-consuming passion I'd felt for Erik, but it hadn't lasted. He said I was too distant; I said I was simply mature. We said our goodbyes and the whole thing was drama free and very adult. I silently patted myself on the back. I'd grown up; I had learned from my mistakes. I was over it, over Erik, and had maintained a stable relationship for a period of time and not fallen apart when it was over. It felt like a success. A hollow, lonely success, but still...success. And then one night at 3:00 a.m....Erik texted me. We had devolved to texting each other only on our birthdays and at Christmas. Simple, empty texts, good wishes and nothing more than you'd tell a stranger at Starbucks. It was safer that way, better than dredging up the past, better than fighting. Better than never speaking again.

Then there was the 3:00 a.m. text, followed by my teasing response. I thought that would be it, but the next night, he texted again. It wasn't 3:00 a.m., it was a little after nine and I was already in bed, reading the latest Stephen King. I glanced over at my phone, expecting a text from the guy I had been dating, as we were still friends (imagine that!) and planning to see a movie over the weekend. I entertained a thought that we might get back together again, that he might be right and I had been distant, but I dismissed it. No, I was done trying to conform and please someone else. I was feeling cocky, until I looked at my phone.

I miss you all the time. I would like to see you. Please?

My heart was trip-hammering in my chest even before I got to the "Please?" Maybe I wasn't as over Erik as I thought I was. I hesitated. Should I see him? It was the first time since that missed concert that he'd asked to see me. I considered dashing off a quick rejection, telling him I was seeing someone. But that seemed like a game we would've played when we were together. I didn't want to play games, but that didn't stop me from putting my phone down and reading another thirty pages of my novel while my mind worked out how I should really respond.

Okay, I texted back an hour later. *When?*

He didn't wait an hour. Less than a minute later my phone vibrated, as if he'd been holding his phone in his hand waiting for me. His response put the ball firmly in my court. *Whenever you're available. Just give me a date, time and location and I'll be there.*

I laughed out loud. That didn't sound like the Erik I knew. Warning bells went off. What did he want? Booty call, I thought again. No, that wasn't his style, either. At least not with me.

I didn't know what to say and I didn't want to say something I'd regret in the morning. *I'll check my calendar and text you tomorrow.* That seemed fair. It wasn't a game; I needed time to think.

Thank you, Fiona.

I fell asleep and dreamed of him and the next morning I gave him a date, time and location. I hoped I wouldn't regret it.

"You look amazing," he said four days later as he sat across from me at a new Mexican restaurant that had just opened the previous month. I'd deliberately chosen a place we had never been together before, not wanting to open the can of worms that was the many bad memories between us.

"Thanks! You—" I trailed off. He didn't look amazing. He looked unbelievably thin and haggard. "You look happy," I finished lamely, though his big smile did suggest happiness, even if it didn't quite reach his eyes.

He laughed. "I look like hell and I know it. But thanks. I'm happy to see you."

We placed our orders. I demurred when the waiter suggested a margarita and settled for a Coke. I wanted to keep my wits about me with Erik.

"So what's up?"

He laughed, and it sounded good. Too good. "That's the Fiona I know and—" His smile faded. "Yeah, well, it's a fair question. I needed to see you. Life has been...tough lately and you were always a rock for me."

I was literally biting the inside of my jaw at this. A big point of contention between us had been that I was always there for him but he didn't, or couldn't, return the favor. We were different like that—me the nurturer, him the one happy to let me nurture him no matter how much it depleted my own reserves.

"What's going on?" I honestly didn't want to ask. I didn't want to be dragged into whatever drama he was in the midst of. I had a thought—what if it was about a girl? What if what had precipitated his texts had been a need for relationship advice? That would explain the first late-night text—fighting with a girlfriend, reminding him of his ex. I literally groaned. "Please don't tell me you need me to sort out a problem with a girl for you. Seriously."

He looked at me wide-eyed. "You think I'd ask you to meet me for that? *Seriously?*"

I spread my hands wide, wishing I'd gone for the margarita after all. "Sorry. This is all kind of...unexpected."

"There's no girl problem, Fiona," he said. "I have dated, yes, I was seeing someone for a while and it didn't work out, if you want to know the truth..."

I shook my head, feeling myself getting angry. "Enough. I got it. You're out there dating. Good for you."

"That wasn't my point." He sounded as calm and patient as he had when he sat down. "I just wanted you to know I didn't want to see you because I needed you to fix my love life. In fact, I didn't want to see you to fix anything. Promise. In fact, it's the opposite. Or whatever the opposite is of needing to be fixed. I'm good now. I'm okay. It's been hell, but I'm okay. That's why I wanted to see you."

"What happened?" I asked, exasperated by now. I just wanted to know. "Are you dying?"

"No, but my dad did."

I'm pretty sure my jaw hit the table. I gaped at him for a long minute, no trace of humor on his face. He was serious.

"Oh my god. What happened, Erik?" I asked quietly. "What's going on?"

"Massive stroke right after Christmas. He was just in the kitchen making pancakes one Sunday morning and the next minute...he was gone. It's been rough on my mom, not having anyone close by. So, well, I'm moving to Chicago to be closer to her. I've already put in some applications at schools there."

My mind was reeling. Erik's dad, his idol, had died. He was moving to Chicago. I didn't even know what to say or how to process all that, so I went for the easiest.

"School? You're going back to school?"

He laughed. "That's what you ask about?"

"I figured I'd start small."

"Wise woman, always." Our dinner had arrived by now, but I honestly didn't think I could eat a bite. I couldn't stop staring at him. "Yes, I'm going to back to school. To be a teacher."

"You want to be a teacher?" I knew I sounded like a parrot, but I couldn't help myself. I felt like I didn't know this man sitting in front of me. We'd met when my downstairs neighbor in my apartment building had started a grease fire. Erik, looking like the stereotypical hot fireman, had shown up on my doorstep to evacuate me to safety. Of course, the fire had been contained to my neighbor's stove, but still...it was the kind of meet cute that made for a great cocktail party conversation. And now Erik, the rock-climbing, skydiving, high-octane firefighter was going to be...a teacher?

"Wow," was all I could manage when he laughed at my expression and nodded.

He told me he wanted to follow in his dad's footsteps—he'd been a college professor—and how glad his mom was that he'd be moving back closer to home. We swapped work stories and I didn't even know what else, my mind still in a surreal haze from his bombshell. There were long silences and longer looks and I had the sense of time slipping by and needing to say more, but all I could do was shake my head.

"Wow, this is strange," I said, with a laugh.

"I know it's a lot to take in, and I know maybe it's too late for us, but I thought—"

I really wanted to know what he thought, but the waiter was there to clear our table of the plates I didn't even remember eating from. Once we were alone again and Erik was signing the check, I found myself panicking. Dinner was over, and other than some small talk about me, and his laundry list of life changes, we'd not really said much. I didn't know what I wanted to say, but I knew I wasn't ready for this—whatever *this* was—to end.

"Want to come over to my place?" I asked, a little too quickly, as he followed me out to the parking lot. I sounded spooked, and I was. Erik...two years gone from my life, but never quite gone-gone, until now. Knowing he'd be hundreds of miles away suddenly made our breakup seem that much more final. "I feel like there's more to say than just goodbye."

If he thought that was corny, he didn't show it. He nodded. "I was hoping you'd ask."

A week that had started with me not having seen Erik in two years was ending with him following me home. My head was still spinning—no margarita necessary—when I let us into my place. This was the last thing I had expected to happen, him coming over, so my apartment wasn't exactly spotless. I nudged the cat out of the way and straightened as I went from front door to kitchen.

"Can I get you a drink?" I asked, hoping my voice didn't sound as shaky as I felt.

"I'm not really thirsty." He had followed me and I found his close proximity unnerving. "And I'm guessing neither are you."

I wasn't. I was just going through the motions. And while I didn't intend to be playing a game, it felt like I was. "Nope. Not at all. I don't know what the hell I'm doing, actually."

He looked at me, blinked, and started laughing. That made me laugh. Pretty soon, we were both doubled over in laughter and the cat had fled for the bedroom. None of it was funny and nothing made sense, but one minute we were laughing and the next minute he had his arms around me and was kissing me— and there was nothing at all funny about that, either.

"God, I missed you," he murmured against my lips. "So much."

"Me, too." I didn't want to talk. I didn't want to think. And when it dawned on me that I wasn't talking or thinking, I put my hand against his chest and firmly pushed him away. "But what are we doing?"

He stared at me, his breathing a little ragged, as was mine. "I don't know. I swear, this wasn't what I intended." He held up his hands as if to ward me off. "I really didn't think we'd do anything but have dinner and catch up and—"

He trailed off for the second time in explaining what we were doing. This time, there was no waiter to interrupt. "And?" I prompted. "What did you want tonight to be about?"

"Honestly?"

I rolled my eyes as I leaned against the counter, putting as much space between us as I could in my small kitchen. It would've been easy enough to relocate to the couch in the living room, but I was tired of interruptions. I wanted to know what was going on in his head.

"No, lie to me."

He sighed. "Yeah, well...I thought tonight would be about... starting over."

It was a good thing we'd already eaten dinner, or I surely would have choked on my enchilada. "Starting over? You and me? Seriously?"

"Seriously."

I needed to sit down, but the only way out of the kitchen was to nudge past him in the doorway and I wasn't getting that close. "But...you're moving. To Chicago. Soon."

He nodded.

"But you were hoping we'd start over tonight?"

He nodded again. "I know it doesn't make sense—"

I laughed. "Math doesn't make sense. Politics doesn't make sense. This, this is just crazy talk."

"So you don't want to?" His expression said it all. He was hurt. "You're really over me?"

I shook my head. "It doesn't matter! You're moving, remember? Moving. Whatever this might be"—I gestured to the space between us—"doesn't matter. You're leaving."

My voice had risen with every word until I was practically shouting. I took a deep breath and said, very softly, "And no,

I'm not over you. Obviously."

He laughed again, and it changed his entire look. I liked it. "It's only Chicago, Fiona. Seriously. My dad's death hit me hard—look at me."

I had been looking for the past couple of hours, but I did as he said. There were lines around his eyes I didn't remember, a crease in his forehead that made him look pensive and older than he was. And the weight loss didn't help.

"You look...not good."

"I know. And honestly, I look better than I did a couple of months ago," he said with a wry grin. "I *feel* better, too. Because I've had time to come to terms with Dad's death and realize that I was kind of floating along in life, not really doing anything meaningful. Not really pursuing what I want for myself."

"And what do you want for yourself?"

"You."

I looked away. It's what I wanted to hear, but that didn't make it true. "Yeah?"

"Yeah. You, but not just you. I want to be there for my mom because she and dad were there for me my whole life. I want to be a teacher. I'm glad I've been a firefighter, glad for the training and the experience, but I want to do something that makes me feel like I'm making a difference every day and not just when there's an emergency. I want to trade in the balls-to-the-wall adrenaline rush for something more consistent and stable and, well, adult."

"Adult, huh?"

"Yeah, Fiona. It was time for me to grow up and figure out what I want, and I want you. The only adrenaline rush I want is the one I get when I'm close to you." He closed that short distance between us and took me in his arms.

My mind was spinning and I had nowhere to go, nowhere to look, except in his very earnest, very familiar eyes. I had missed him in a way I'd wanted to deny and that point was driven home by the moisture collecting between my thighs and the way I wanted to press my body against every inch of him, especially the bulge in his pants that was unmistakable. He was thinner, but the muscles were still there, flexing and holding me close as if I might run. But I had no desire to run; I was exactly where I had wanted to be. It was as if two years hadn't passed at all, but in another way it was as if he were a stranger I needed to discover.

"Bedroom, now," was all I could mutter as I reached up to press my lips to his. I didn't want to think anymore. Later, I would think later. But right now, there was an urge growing in me. A need only Erik could satisfy.

He took my hand and I followed him into my bedroom. The bed wasn't made, but instead of looking messy it simply looked inviting—as if it were waiting for us and had taken the time to turn back the spread and rumple the sheets so we would feel welcome. Erik tumbled me down lengthwise across the mattress and I fell willingly, aching for him.

Clothes came off a piece at a time, with each of us working to help the other. Naked. I wanted him naked, I wanted to feel his skin against mine. I caught my breath as I stared at his body; the weight loss looked unnatural on his muscular frame and it brought forth some deep protective urge in me. I wanted to feed him, fatten him up, bring him back to me. But first, god, I just wanted to fuck him.

I didn't need an invitation to straddle him and press my wet slit against the length of his erection. He let out a groan that was as full of need and longing as I was feeling and I knew I was home. Slowly, I slid down his shaft, taking first the head then the entire length of him inside me. *Yes.* It had been a long time, but my body still remembered him, still tightened as he filled me, knowing his shape, remembering the way he filled me just so.

"God, I've missed you," he said through gritted teeth, his breath already ragged. "I've thought about you, about this, so much. I should never have let you go. But I didn't know how to keep you."

I didn't say anything. My brain couldn't form the words to say what I was feeling, what I wanted. All I could do was show him. And I did. Leaning over his lanky body, I kissed him, using my lips and tongue and teeth while my pussy tightened on his cock and I rode him. He gripped my ass, holding tight while I moved on him, groaning into my mouth with every downward thrust. His tongue swept along mine, teasing out my own breathy moans as he slid his hands over the curve of my hips, up my waist and around to cup my breasts and thumb my nipples. The movements, the feelings, were familiar as a recurring dream— but there was something more, something new, about the way we connected. We found a rhythm that was harder, faster, more immediate. His hands stroked up and down my curves from breast to hips as he rose to meet my downward thrusts.

My orgasm surprised me. I was so caught up in watching his expression, enjoying the way his body responded to me, that one moment I was there, solid and present and completely focused on riding his erection and drawing forth his moans that mirrored my own, and the next I was flying to pieces, feeling breathless and weightless as my climax pulled me apart and Erik's thrusts became the center of my world. I cried out as he held me to him and I belatedly realized he was right there with me in the midst of his own orgasm that left his body taut and quivering. I stroked my hand down his chest as I shifted off him, my head still fitting so well in the hollow of his shoulder. He played with the damp wisps of my hair as I continued to soothe him with a gentle hand.

"Wow," he said finally when his breath had returned to normal.

I laughed. "That word is getting a lot of play tonight. That was...unexpected."

"Yeah, but I can't say it wasn't what I was hoping for."

"You said you weren't expecting this," I said, inhaling the heady scent of our lovemaking.

"Doesn't mean a guy can't hope."

We were quiet for a while, and I wondered if he was attempting to process all of this madness with the same rapid-fire speed as I was. Probably not. I am notorious for overthinking things, and though he'd laid a lot on me at once and then fucked me sense- less, I was trying not to make it more complicated than it was. But it *was* complicated, no two ways about it. And in the after- math of the mind-blowing sex, my rational mind was trying to make sense of it all.

"So, Chicago, huh?"

"Yeah. Not for a couple of months, though. I have a lot of loose ends to tie up," he said, his fingertips stroking along my hairline, teasing the shell of my ear.

I swallowed hard past the lump in my throat. "Am I a loose end?"

"No, I told you—you're part of my plans for the future. If you'll have me."

"I see. And how do you imagine this working, with you in Chicago?"

He laughed, his chest rumbling with that happy sound, and it made me smile. "I don't know. I'm flying by the seat of my pants here, Fi. I just know what I want and that I'm going to do whatever it takes to get it."

"Long-distance relationship?"

"Sure, why not? It's just a few hours by car. I've socked away a lot of savings and I have financial aid and grants, so I won't need to work right away. And I will have all kinds of time during school breaks. You have vacation time. We can meet halfway;

I'll come here, whatever I need to do."

He made it sound so easy. I was torn between elation and hopelessness. Could we make it work this time? Was it worth the risk? The answer was in the curve of his smile and the warmth of his body pressed against mine. Yeah, it was worth it.

"Okay," I said, though there were a thousand questions I wanted to ask. Keep it simple, right? "Okay."

He rolled over me, covering my body with his own, and I felt the press of his erection returning. The questions and doubts fled and all that mattered was this moment. We'd figure out the rest later.

ABOUT THE AUTHORS

LAILA BLAKE (lailablake.com) is an author, linguist and translator. She writes character-driven love stories, cofounded the micropublishing venture Lilt Literary and blogs about feminism and society. Laila's body of work encompasses literary erotica, romance and speculative fiction. Her short stories have been featured in numerous anthologies.

JILLIAN BOYD (ladylaidbare.com) is the author of numerous erotic short stories and has been published by the likes of Cleis Press, House of Erotica and Constable and Robinson. She lives with her adorable boyfriend in London, where she blogs, bakes and dreams about wild, uninhibited romance while hanging the laundry.

RACHEL KRAMER BUSSEL (rachelkramerbussel.com) is the editor of *The Big Book of Orgasms; Cheeky Spanking Stories; Flying High: Sexy Stories from the Mile High Club; Irresistible: Erotic Romance for Couples* and more. She writes about sex, dating, books and pop culture, teaches erotic writing work-shops and tweets @raquelita.

Born in one country, raised in a second and living in a third, **J. CRICHTON** is a teacher and translator who uses her jet-setting experiences as inspiration for steamy writing. She is a firm believer in chasing dreams, happy endings and great sex.

CLAIRE DE WINTER is a published novelist and recovering attorney. She lives in the industrial Midwest with her husband and two small children.

EMERALD's erotic fiction has been featured in anthologies published by Cleis Press, Mischief and Logical-Lust. She's an assistant newsletter editor and Facebook group moderator for Marketing for Romance Writers (MFRW) and blogs about sexu-ality from psychological, social and spiritual perspectives at her website, The Green Light District (TheGreenLightDistrict.org).

TAMSIN FLOWERS (tamsinflowers.com) writes lighthearted erotica, often with a twist in the tale and a sense of fun. Her stories have appeared in numerous anthologies and usually, she's working on at least ten stories at once.

MIA HOPKINS is a Los Angeles-based writer of romance and erotic fiction. Her work has been featured by Clean Sheets, Go Deeper Press, and Cleis Press. If she had a choice, her death row meal would be oysters, whiskey, a baguette, and a giant cake with bolt cutters baked inside.

SKYLAR KADE (skylarkade.com) writes erotic romance, usually of the kinky persuasion. She lives in California and spends her time asking the cabana boys to bring her more mimosas and feed her strawberries while she dreams up her next naughty adventure.

H. KEYES is an art aficionado and punk rocker living in Japan. She's into design, tattoos, kimono, decadent history and window-shopping all around Tokyo.

RENEE LUKE is a multi-published award-winning author, who has written for several houses, but is now self-publishing. She writes stories with rich texture, deep emotions and realist characters. She creates stories where sensual seduces erotic and believes in love, romance and happily-ever-afters.

KIM STRATTFORD (kimstrattford.com) lives in Northern Virginia with two cats and a whole cast of characters in her head. She has stories accepted to *Powerless Against You: A Romantic Superhero Anthology* from New Mourning Publishing and Roane Publishing's *Summer's Embrace* anthology.

ALEX TOBIN (tobinwords.com) lives in Portland, OR, with a huge collection of great books and terrible movies. When not dreaming of the grand marketing scheme that will bring his works to the attention of the world, Alex can be found procrastinating about writing and laughing in the face of looming deadlines.

ABOUT
THE EDITOR

Described by The Romance Reader as "a budding force to be reckoned with" and as one of the "legendary erotica heavy-hitters" by Violet Blue, **KRISTINA WRIGHT** (kristinawright.com) is an award-winning author and the editor of over a dozen Cleis Press anthologies, including *Fairy Tale Lust* and the Best Erotic Romance series. Her short fiction has appeared in over one hundred anthologies and her nonfiction has appeared in publications as diverse as *USA Today*, the *Washington Post*, *Cosmopolitan*, Narratively and *Brain, Child Magazine*. She is the author of the groundbreaking cross-genre relationship guide *Bedded Bliss: A Couple's Guide to Lust Ever After* and the HarperCollins erotic romance *Seduce Me Tonight*. She holds degrees in English and humanities from Charleston Southern University and Old Dominion University and has taught English and world mythology at the college level. She lives in Virginia with her husband, a retired lieutenant commander in the Navy, and their two young sons.